Silent Day in Tangier

Also by Tahar Ben Jelloun, published by Quartet Books:

Solitaire
The Sand Child
The Sacred Night (winner of the Prix Goncourt)

Silent Day in Tangier

Tahar Ben Jelloun

Translated by David Lobdell

QUARTET BOOKS

First published in Great Britain by
Quartet Books Limited 1991
A member of the Namara Group
27/29 Goodge Street
London W1P 1FD

This edition published by arrangement with
Harcourt Brace Jovanovich Inc., Orlando, USA

A CIP record for this book is
available from the British Library

Printed and bound in Great Britain by
BPCC Hazell Books
Aylesbury, Bucks, England
Member of BPCC Ltd.

For my father

"Time is an old man infected with the malice of a child."

Georges Schéhadé,
L'Emigré de Brisbane

T his is the story of a man led astray by the wind, forgotten by time, and scorned by death.

The wind comes from the east in this city where the Atlantic and the Mediterranean meet, a city built on a succession of hills and wrapped in legend—a pleasant, ineffable enigma of a city.

The events begin with the century, or thereabouts. They form a triangle in the life of this man, who, at an early age—he was twelve or thirteen at the time—left Fez to find work in the Rif, first at Nador and then at Melilla, returned to Fez during the war, then emigrated in the fifties with his small family to Tangier, a seaport in the perpetual grip of the wind, a city in which indolence and ingratitude reign supreme.

Death is a vessel carried in the hands of young women neither beautiful nor ugly; they move to and fro in a ramshackle house, past the disbelieving, suspicious gaze of the one who steadily rejects them.

At the moment, he is in bed. He is bored. He would like to go out, to cross the city, or part of it, on foot, to stop at the Grand Socco and buy some bread, to open his shop and resume work on his djellabas, cutting them from long bolts of white fabric. But a severe bout of bronchitis has forced him to take to his bed, and the East Wind, with its rain squalls, is even more persuasive than the doctor's instructions. The house is very cold. The dampness has left patterns of green mold on the walls. The moisture on the windowpanes drips down the wooden frames, which are slowly rotting.

Wrapped in a burnous and a woolen blanket, he thinks, he dozes, he listens to the rain, no longer knowing what to do with himself in this narrow bed that his body has transformed into a kind of trap, which will open one day to send him plunging into the wet black earth. It is the bed that protects him; it is the bed that keeps him imprisoned. When he gets up, he is so shaky he can barely stay on his feet;

so he gets back in bed, recalling how he was once able to climb the mountain road of Al-Huceima with a sack on his back that weighed at least forty-five pounds. He conjures up the image of a young man who had to go to work after the death of his father, a young man left to look after nearly a dozen siblings in an ancient house in the medina of Fez. The memory is a painful one, but it fills him with pride. It was in such circumstances that he learned the meaning of self-respect and discovered that adversity need not be seen as a curse.

But these recurring memories have begun to bore him, like the white sky glimpsed through the window and the wind that blows around the house and slams the doors.

The boredom derives from the annoying repetition of things, the same images endlessly revived and impoverished through use. The boredom derives from the immobility of the objects surrounding his bed, many of which are as old as he; worn-out objects that are always there, always in their place, serviceable and silent. Time passes with aggravating slowness. The cleaning woman washes the floor, ignoring his presence, humming to herself as she works, as if she were alone in the room. He watches her, conscious of his helplessness, resisting the temptation to ask her to make a little less noise. He tells himself she wouldn't understand. She comes from the outskirts of the city, where those who joined the exodus from the countryside live huddled together along congested streets. She does not appeal to him in the least. He looks at her and asks himself what she is doing in his house. She's young and strong; there is no chance that she will find herself confined to bed by illness. And if she were ill, she wouldn't be alone; she would have her whole family around her, as well as her acquaintances, her neighbors, her friends. He would like to see his children, too—but not around his bed. That's an ill omen; he hasn't reached that point yet. His sickness is not serious; the family must not be alerted. It would be premature, he tells himself. Besides, he likes to have his family around him only on holidays, on joyful occasions. For now, he must concentrate on shaking off this bronchitis. But the boredom, the solitude, the slow, heavy passage of time—these are more intolerable than any illness. His neighbors are not his friends; they are only neighbors, neither good nor bad. He can't invite them in for an hour of small talk; they wouldn't understand. They would have difficulty thinking of something to say to an old man who is sick and bored to death with himself. He, on the other hand, would have a great many things to tell them. But they would only laugh at him. Why should they take the time to listen to a stranger? Oh, it isn't as if they don't know him. Sometimes they hear him when he flies into a rage, or is in the grip of an asthma attack. Four times a day, they see him pass in the alley, as punctual as clockwork. When they fail to hear his footsteps in the morning, they tell themselves that he must be confined to bed. Then they hear his cough, a shrill hacking sound that fills the air around them. They may even catch a glimpse of him from their terraces. Yes, there he is, leaning against a bush, one hand clasped to his chest, trying to bring up the thick mucus that is clogging his windpipe. He expels a long stream of whitish phlegm, then glances nervously to left and right, hoping no one has seen him. He doesn't like this wretched state into which he has fallen; he finds it demeaning, dehumanizing.

No, the neighbors cannot be summoned to keep him company; the men are at work, and the women are busy with the housework and the cooking. He is certainly not going to stoop to inviting the woman next door to come and listen to him reminisce about the war years in Nador and Melilla. If only she were beautiful! But it's out of the question anyway; that sort of thing is not done.

The boredom derives also from the inordinately low ceiling, which has a crack running down its center and threatens at any moment to collapse. From his bed he gazes at it for so long that he imagines he is looking at the sky: a dark, cloudless sky, beneath which a number of familiar and unfamiliar faces bend over him to bid him good-bye. When he turns over, he finds himself facing a wall eroded by dampness, a wall that advances slowly in his direction, coming a little closer each day. He sees it moving, but he can do nothing to stop it, to hold it back. Then he begins to cough, a dry, heaving sound that comes from some place deep in his chest and that causes him to gasp for breath. Painful though it is, the coughing is the only thing that delivers him from these moments of hallucinating anguish. He closes his eyes—not to sleep, but to cut himself off from the walls and the ceiling. He dozes off, seated in a cross-legged position, his head resting in his hands. But suddenly he is jolted to his senses as his body is shaken with coughing, the result of having inadvertently swallowed the wrong way. Even when his health is good, he has difficulty swallowing. He is apt to choke on the slightest thing: his saliva, a gulp of water, a grain of semolina. This is due to a malformation of his throat, a characteristic he shares with other members of his family. One of his brothers, long gone, could never drink a glass of water in a single gulp; he was obliged to swallow it in little mouthfuls. And one of his nephews was nicknamed "the hurrier," because of his tendency to gulp his food and to gasp for breath between each mouthful. In his family, the anguish of aging and dying manifests itself in a congested throat brought on by dangerous choking. Those who swallow the wrong way are those who spend their lives running after money, those who are known for their avarice. They want to ingest everything in a single gulp, amassing wealth and possessions, and doing everything in their power to hold onto them.

Seated on the bed, he takes little sips from a glass of tea. He feels a little better today, but it is still not possible for him to go out. He gazes through the window. The little garden he loves so much is drenched with rain. The weeds are gaining the upper hand out there. On the first nice day, he will have to go out and work in the garden. He asks the cleaning woman to switch on the television set. The picture is not very clear; his eyesight must be deteriorating. It's an American film, dubbed into French. He has trouble understanding it. Why does Moroccan television, which begins the day with the national anthem and a reading from the Koran, devote so much of its time to American and French serials? He feels not only excluded but swindled. The films about cowboys, gangsters, and rich, decadent Americans mean nothing to him. Ordinarily, he remains indifferent to these programs, which are clearly intended for another audience; he may make an ironic comment, criticize some detail, even damn all the "uncultivated, illiterate people of the earth"; but that is generally as far as he will go. But today boredom has got the better of him, making him more irritable than usual. He shakes his fist at the television set, for which he paid more than eight thousand dirhams—money that might as well have been thrown into the sea.

Whom might he call to come and keep him company? What friend could he invite to come and chat with him, to help him pass the time a little less painfully? Not just anyone will do. Otherwise, he could engage the services of a nurse or a paid companion. But he has no intention of doing that. He isn't sick; he doesn't see himself as a sick man. He is merely prevented from going outdoors by the accursed East Wind and a sky full of dirty rain clouds.

His friends were once too numerous to count, but they are almost all gone now. He recalls them, one by one, and cannot suppress his resentment at the fact that they departed sooner than expected. Their disappearance has resulted in this solitude that weighs so heavily on him today. He feels justified in being offended by their cruel abandonment of him, after so many shared experiences, after so many good times and bad times. Even his brothers, Tahar, Driss, and Muhammad, who could not exactly be counted among his friends but whom he loved nonetheless, are dead now. He buried them, one after the other, weeping each time like a child all alone in a corner. For a while, he made an attempt to keep in touch with his nephews and nieces. But there, too, he met with nothing but disappointment.

His thoughts turn to Moulay Ali. A large, jovial man, a bon vivant. A merchant who, at the age of sixty-five, decided to retire, as if he were just another civil servant, and spend the remainder of his days in idleness. Following the death of his wife, a foreigner, he reorganized his life. Then chance led him to marry again, this time an aristocratic woman who was past the childbearing age. They lived peacefully together. And they were discreet neighbors. Moulay Ali spent his afternoons playing cards with his friends, men of independent means who were also retired, and who always wore white, as if they were going to a wedding. They played *tute*, a game that dated back to the Andalusian era and in which the cards still bore their original Spanish names: *Rey, Espada, Copas*. Each player was given ten cards. The aim of the game was to make purchases with the points you held in your hand. It was a game that unleashed passions, ranging from quasi-epileptic agitation at one end of the scale to euphoria and unrestrained joy at the other. It is said that some husbands forfeited their wives, having offered them as collateral in the game—but that was before his time.

Moulay Ali played for pleasure and for the joy of being surrounded by his friends. But one day, when he was at the mosque, he suffered a heart attack. He was rushed to the hospital. When he regained consciousness, the first thing he asked the doctor for was permission to play cards in the afternoon. His companions came to play with him on his hospital bed, making as little noise as possible, in order not to attract the attention of the staff. On that day,

Moulay Ali made his friends promise that when he died they would play a game of *tute* beside his coffin. No one had the courage to refuse him.

A few months later, Moulay Ali was struck down by another heart attack, in the middle of a card game. Before dying, and even as he raised the index finger of his right hand to utter the traditional Muslim profession of faith, "There is no God but Allah, and Muhammad is his prophet," he brandished a card in his left hand to remind his friends of their promise. They did not play in the presence of the coffin, but for three days they played a round of *tute* in their usual spot, their hearts heavy, their eyes brimming with tears.

The rain is still falling. From his bed, he can see a corner of the roof of Moulay Ali's house. His thoughts dwell on that man, with whom he never had the pleasure of playing cards but to whom he spoke from time to time, reminiscing about the years spent in the Rif. Moulay Ali was a man who never knew solitude or boredom, who never knew what it was to grow old. Even though he lived into his seventies, he never knew a day of sickness or infirmity. He was a good neighbor. If he were still alive, he would come and spend a few hours at his friend's bedside. But he was gone, and his companions had no reason these days to enter the home of the aristocratic woman, who continued to lead a simple, discreet life.

With his index finger he makes a cross in the air to expunge the name of Moulay Ali; then he lies gazing at a photograph hanging on the opposite wall of the room. It is a photograph of Touizi, a man who never married; he died while running after a beautiful young woman. Touizi led a life that was the envy of all his friends, and of all the husbands and fathers. Single by choice, devoted to pleasure, he moved from one adventure to another with wives of other men and with a bevy of naive young women attracted by his good looks and his generosity. Secretary of an Eastern prince, he had few responsibilities, and looking after the affairs of his often absent employer did not overtax him. So he was able to devote most of his time to the seduction of women, the pursuit of the good life, and telling his companions about his many exploits. He claimed that the best time to make love was between the hour of four-o'clock prayers and sunset. He was able to speak at great length on such matters as the arousal of the female body, the use of natural light, and how to tell when a woman was about to reach a climax. For him, the night was made for sleeping, for allowing the body to rest after its long journey through the day; it was the least propitious moment for lovemaking. But the afternoon was a vast open space in the middle of the day that lent itself better to sexual revels than to tedious activities like card games in which the flag of sex flew at half-mast. In a sense, that brief period might be said to fill the entire day: prior to it, you anticipated it with joy and expectation; during it, you took your pleasure; and, after it, you relived the experience in memory as you calmly prepared for the night.

Touizi had an insatiable appetite for the female body. He even allowed himself occasional baseness, which he acknowledged willingly. He declared that he had never been in love with a woman; which would have caused him great pain had he not decided at an early age to devote himself to all women, to spend his life rendering them homage, magnifying their qualities, and celebrating their beauty.

Touizi was a rake. He upset the tranquillity of many a faithful husband with his disturbing accounts of his liaisons. But now that he is no longer here, his friends miss him. In particular this one misses him, so desperate is he for company. He tries to imagine what Touizi would say if he were here now. He would come to visit him at the end of the day, having just made love to a young divorcée. (Touizi avoided virgins, who might involve him in a paternity suit.) As usual, he would take an inordinate delight in recounting his latest adventure in great detail. Without appearing to mean any harm, he might even boast a little, thus provoking his friend's envy. At a certain moment in his life, Touizi, finding himself tempted to marry, had come up with an original though not very practical formula: an endlessly renewable marriage contract! This never failed to prompt his friends' laughter. But now Touizi is gone. It was inconsiderate of him to take his leave so abruptly. What did he die of, exactly? No one is sure, but it's not hard to imagine him running after a veiled woman, stumbling on a stone, falling, splitting his skull open on the edge of the sidewalk. But perhaps he was killed by a cuckolded husband—throttled, castrated. No, that was too ugly! The image of such bloodshed in this room, on this long afternoon, accompanied by the sounds of Touizi's moans and pleas for help, is too much for an old man to contemplate. It is more agreeable to imagine Touizi dying a natural death after making love, collapsing in the arms of a young woman who had never set eyes on him before that day. He'd gone too far, he hadn't known when to stop. He died a peaceful death, having paid final magnificent homage to a woman's body. Had he been a little more cautious, had he lived a little less recklessly and smoked a little less, he might have lived longer. Had he looked after himself, he might still be here today, enjoying life, enchanting his friends with his stories.

Bachir died at prayer. No two men leave the world in exactly the same way. He remembers the days when Bachir used to come to visit him in his shop, eager to discuss the latest political developments in the Arab world. A passionate devotee of Islam, he never disguised his disappointment with all those Arabs he deemed unworthy of their heritage. He never missed a prayer or a film; after he stopped working, he divided his time between the cinema and the mosque. A cultivated man, he had one of the best libraries in the city, in which works on Islam, in Arabic and French, were as numerous as books of poetry. An intellectual who was completely at home in both languages, he had undertaken to revive the tradition of the enlightened Arab who is conversant with a number of languages and cultures. He was a man who had no time for idle talk. Whenever he visited the shop, it was either to communicate some important piece of news or to expound upon the significance of a study recently undertaken in London or Vienna that he had learned about through a report on a foreign radio station. But then he died while at prayer, a healthy man who had left open on his desk a book he had recently been consulting. It was a fine death, if a little too sudden and unexpected.

The cleaning woman brings him tea. He glares at her, muttering under his breath. The tea is lukewarm and not as sweet as he likes it. This is enough to put him in a rage. He calls for the woman. She takes her time in coming. He shouts. She enters the room, mumbling excuses. She picks up the tray containing the tea and asks if he would like a fresh pot. No; he wants a cup of strong coffee. He curses her. Either she doesn't hear him or she prefers to feign deafness. She's a poor woman who has to work hard to make a living—even if her primary duty is to put up with his moodiness. He sips his coffee and plunges back into his morbid thoughts. "That's life," he says to himself. A life that has eliminated all his friends, one after the other. A vast empty space has been created around him. He thinks of Allam, who lay dying for weeks in a hospital bed. Cirrhosis of the liver. Imagine, a man who never drank! Poor Allam didn't have an evil bone in his body. He was a funny man, too, who liked telling stories. And he hated work. His wife was rich, a fact that didn't displease him. He referred to her as "the patron." His friends were inclined to scorn him because he allowed himself to be ruled by a woman.

Poor Allam knew suffering only once in his life, and that was when death overtook him. It approached him, hovered over him for a week or so, then carried him off in a wave of excruciating pain.

When he had visited Allam in his hospital room, he couldn't hold back his tears, because he knew he would never see his friend again. Today, he is troubled by the picture he took away of that man. How can he not see himself in Allam's place, lying on those rough white sheets, in those moments of complete loneliness, with nothing to supply his desperate need for consolation and peace? So many images have come to haunt him on this long winter afternoon. How can he escape them? His children are far away: one lives outside the country, where he cannot be disturbed (he would come if he were summoned, but one must not exaggerate the need); the other has an important position and cannot leave without a serious reason. Now, there is clearly nothing serious enough to bring him to his father's side on this day— nothing but a lonely old man lying beneath a leaden sky that is slowly descending and will at any moment pass through the roof and come to rest on his chest. How can he escape the blind force that presses on his rib cage and that fills his head with horrible scenes of suffering patients lying in hospital beds beneath the glittering eyes of death? Ah, if only some lovely young woman would come to pay him a visit, rub his back, caress his hands, spread her long, perfumed hair over his body. That would be so nice. Unless, of course, she wore the blank face of death. One of his cousins, who had had a brush with death, told him that it was just such a superb creature who hovered over him as he was about to die, beckoning to him, urging him to join her. In her impatience, she lost her balance as she reached out to take him by the hand, and toppled into the void.

It occurs to him that he could call Abbas, his former accomplice in joking about others. But they are no longer on speaking terms. The last time they saw each other, they got into an argument and exchanged insults. That was more than a year ago—no, a year ago to the day. Perhaps this might serve as a pretext to invite the man to make peace? They have similar temperaments: both are inclined to be facetious and ironic. But the moment one turns his ironic gaze on the other, the atmosphere darkens and the victim flies into a rage.

No; his pride won't allow him to call Abbas. And yet he feels that it would do him good to exchange a few jokes at someone else's expense. It would alleviate his sadness a little, and the afternoon would not seem so terribly long. But whom could they hold up to ridicule? All their friends, all their victims, are dead. Surely they wouldn't go so far as to speak ill of the dead? Yes, they might even do that. It is not unpleasant to imagine settling accounts with certain departed ones.

What has become of Abbas? He has two wives, two households, a number of children. And his business is thriving. At one point, he tried to take a third wife, a young widow who worked in his store, but his two wives get together to oppose him, and he had to abandon the idea. This did not prevent him from sitting in his Mercedes outside the local schoolyard and ogling the girls as they came out. On one occasion, his nearsightedness played a trick on him, and he followed his own daughter, who was walking home with a friend. When she turned around accusingly, he muttered something about wanting to make sure she was behaving. But that evening he made the mistake of giving her a gift, and she realized immediately that he was trying to buy her silence. The story quickly made the rounds of the neighborhood, with the result that poor Abbas had to not only change his glasses but give up hanging around the local schoolyards.

Outside, the wind is howling, sovereign and indifferent. How is a man to escape time? How can he make it less oppressive? How can he rid his thoughts of it? How can he conjure up a beautiful young woman, her lithe body crossing the line of his vision, caressing the eyes of an old man who despite everything is still in command of his faculties, who refuses to submit to the slow breakdown of the senses and pours his medicine into the toilet, then gives the chain a violent pull, as if to remove forever all traces of it.

Delving deeper into his memory, he recalls an autumn afternoon in Melilla when a young Spanish woman offered herself to him in the back of his shop. An innocent, shy creature, she had decided to defy her Catholic parents in this way, because she was irritated by their forever warning her against men, in particular *los mauros*. He was a fine figure of a man in those days, elegant and refined. Even today, he enjoys looking at the photographs taken when he dressed like a European and spent his evenings in private Spanish clubs to which few Muslims were admitted. Those were days of seduction and pleasure, of cards and drink. In those long-ago days, he imbibed more than a few glasses of sherry and enjoyed more than a few clandestine affairs with Spanish women. There was Lola, who came to the shop from time to time, always unannounced. The moment he caught sight of her, he would lower the blind on the front window, hoping to evade the prying eyes of his envious neighbors. He would never forget Lola's small, soft, warm breasts! The memory is a very vivid one, even a little painful. A smile of nostalgia spreads over his face, lending a little light to the long, dark afternoon. He was twenty at the time; Lola was barely sixteen. Imagine a minor in the arms of a Muslim! Enough to ruin a man's career! But he enjoyed the risk. Then, one day, Lola married an officer in the colonial army and he never saw her again. Perhaps it was just as well. Where is she today? Dead? No; Lola is immortal. That body, that gaze, those breasts were made for eternity. Besides, she is always sixteen—perhaps twenty. But such thoughts make him doubt her very existence. Perhaps he invented her. And why not? Such things do no harm. He has every right to believe that at the age of twenty he loved and was loved by a beautiful Spanish girl named Lola. He would like to encounter her again in his dreams, but to do that he would have to find a way to sleep without being troubled by his clogged nasal passages, by the sound of air whistling in and out. No; Lola will not come today to slip into his bed and press her naked body to his. He caresses his cheek, pulls at it, fails to get a grip.

There is almost no flesh left on his bones. Lola certainly wouldn't like these wrinkles and this rough, parched skin. Perhaps she is alone today, too—abandoned by her children, confined to a nursing home. Perhaps her husband died during one of the wars. Perhaps she spends her days talking to a cat—abandoned, too. He thinks of all the old people who have been forcibly separated from life, confined to homes conveniently located near a cemetery. Fortunately this kind of "progressive" measure has not yet been introduced in Morocco. His children would never subject him to such an indignity. He gave them a proper upbringing; he taught them that respect for one's parents is second only to respect for God. And the children, even as adults, don't want to lose the blessing of their father or mother. If one of them ever dared to try to remove him from his home, he would curse him and put up a struggle. To place him in a home for the aged would amount to condemning him to an early, bitter death. Dying is never an easy business, but it is unthinkable that a man should have to leave this life with a kick in the backside from his children. He is in no danger of that, since his sons are far away, far from Tangier. When they telephone, which they do fairly regularly, he never complains, he assures them that all is well. He wouldn't want to them worry. If they left their jobs to come to his side, it would be an indication that he was ill. Such a visit would only make matters worse. He mustn't exaggerate.

He reaches out and switches on the little radio. He recognizes the voice of Farid-el-Atrache. He can't stand the man, who doesn't so much sing as lament. "They all lament," he tells himself. Not only are they dull, they're ugly too. It's too much for a man all alone on this interminable afternoon. He's hungry; he should eat something. But he has no appetite for the insipid, spiceless food the doctor has prescribed. Steamed vegetables—no! They're for a sick man, a man on the threshold of death. What he would like is a bowl of well-seasoned *tajine* and beans, with a glass of strong sweet tea to wash it down. But such things are forbidden him. Still, why should he care what the doctor says? He likes to tell the story of one of his friends, given up for dead by the doctor, who expressed the desire to leave this life with a full stomach. The man devoured a large bowl of *tajine* filled with strips of meat simmered in oil, followed by a full pot of tea . . . and promptly recovered! He would like to try the same remedy himself, but his wife refuses to make it for him. His wife is a very disciplined woman; she follows her doctor's instructions to the letter. He teases her about this mercilessly. If she takes her medicine so faithfully, he tells her, it is simply to prove that her illness is a serious one—which he adamantly refuses to believe. This never fails to upset her.

His friends are all dead now, and his family is reduced to a minimum. He is not on particularly good terms with his numerous nephews and cousins. He has been so critical of them and has heaped such scorn on them that he doesn't have the courage to try for reconciliation now that he finds himself in need of human company. He must be consistent. There is one nephew for whom he feels a certain affection, but one he has never spared. They're too much alike—both moralists, critical and impatient. Twenty years separate them. He shudders at the thought of taking instruction from a sixty-year-old man, whom he continues, after all these years, to call "the boy." That would be intolerable, like being murdered in a ruined house.

The image is apt, because his house is falling apart. But he obstinately refuses to acknowledge the cracks in the ceiling and the walls. He could patch them if he wanted to, if only to pass the time. He could call a plumber to repair the leaking faucets, to remove the bits of string he has used here and there, to fix the flush toilet, which never stops running. He could do these things. But he doesn't like plumbers. As far as he's concerned, they are all cheats and impostors. He has never exchanged a single intelligent word with a plumber. He prefers his pieces of string and his leaking faucets. It's not worth the effort to get them repaired. After all, he's been living with them for years now. He and repairmen are not on good terms; it's as simple as that.

What can he do to alleviate his interminable solitude, to dispel the cyclone that whirls endlessly around him and confuses his thoughts? What can he do to bring the sunshine back into his house? Who will lend him the strength to resist, to outwit, the pain? Who will grant him the clearness of mind to go on defying doctors and their infernal medicines? There is one friend he could call: a former bank employee, a man who is retired now but who is still relatively young. They've known one another for years, since they were neighbors in Fez, where the man's father sold Turkish slippers. A good man, like his father before him; not very bright, but amiable enough. At one point, he hoped to make a career in the theater; he even translated *Le bourgeois gentilhomme* into Arabic. The man's name is Larbi, but his stage name was Rabi'e (Spring). When people wanted to make fun of him, they called him Chta' (Winter or Rain). He had to give up his artistic aspirations, finally: there were too many obstacles barring his way. Besides, he was discouraged by the ironic comments of his associates. In moving from the theater to the bank, he lost all trace of his former joie de vivre. He spent his time in the company of older men, married a cousin, and had a number of children.

It is Larbi's wife who answers the phone. He isn't at home; he's away on a trip. Not on tour, no. He has gone to visit his eldest daughter, who has just been appointed to a teaching position in a lycée in Casablanca, in one of those clandestine quarters that spring up overnight unknown to the authorities, where it is so difficult for a young woman on her own to live and work.

The daughter is unmarried, which means that she is still dependent on her family for support. That's normal. But she is lost in the big city. Casablanca is not a place for a young single woman. Larbi has gone to pay her a visit, to lend her a little courage. What bad luck! He should be here to keep his old friend company. Because he too is in need of support, he too is lost and alone. He feels resentful of the poor girl, who is so afraid of being accosted by the riffraff of Casablanca. Why can't she be a little more independent? Why does she have to bother her father, who should keep himself available to those who are in real need of his presence? She might have got married—but no, she is much too particular. She went to the university and accumulated a number of diplomas, so she thinks this gives her the right to be choosy. Is she beautiful, at least? Not really. A little on the heavy side. If she had a husband to look after her, Larbi would be here at this moment, chatting with his old friend. It's a pity, because they understand each other so well. Larbi is a timid, sensitive man; he is patient, he knows how to listen, he doesn't interrupt you every minute or two to say that he has already heard that story three times. No, Larbi doesn't have the impertinence to remind his friend that he is repeating himself. That is a sign of refinement. But he has a daughter who is much less refined. That's how it is, and it's too bad. In the old days, daughters were not sent to school. Beautiful or ugly, they were married off; they were got out of the way. They looked after the house; they had children. Today they still have children, but they have stopped doing the housework. Those who don't marry remain dependent on their fathers. That's normal. But why should she need her father just when his friend is alone and feels he has been abandoned by the whole world? Still, it is impossible for him to be resentful of Larbi. What right would he have to?

"Larbi wouldn't have made a good actor," he tells himself. "Nor would I, for that matter. But at least I can identify a liar and a hypocrite when I see one. He wants to play the role of the good father, but this prevents him from making himself available to his friends. It's a pity. I like him. He's a good man. He smiles at my jokes, even when they're at his expense."

He raises a corner of the curtain and gazes out the window. A wet cat walks by. In his eyes, it symbolizes the complete desolation of this long afternoon. The poor creature looks colder than the cleaning woman, who goes about her work wrapped up in a blanket. He detests the woman. She gets on his nerves. He finds her stupid and ugly. Fortunately, she doesn't attract him. He enjoys mocking her, even in her hearing. "Everything about her is collapsing," he says, "the breasts, the rump, the cheeks, the belly . . ." He resents her for being a woman who lacks everything that might interest him. In his eyes, the good woman is a fraud. Of course, she has to work hard to feed her seven children. So there are moments when he feels a certain pity for her, but he takes great care to conceal it. The cat skirts the wall, trying to keep out of the rain. It's shivering; it must be sick. The East Wind is so strong the little creature has trouble staying on its feet. The wind and the rain are his own worst enemies; they alone are responsible for his asthma and his bronchitis. Why did he ever decide to move to this windswept city? Why did he choose such an unpromising place, where few men have made their fortune and where it is so difficult to make friends? In his case, the friends, the real ones, those who came from Fez or Casablanca, are all dead now. Here in Tangier, they kept in touch with one another because they felt rejected by the natives. If they abandoned Fez, the "city of cities," the mother of culture and savoir-vivre, it was because life there had become impossible, because the city was falling into ruin.

He has never recovered from this move, which took place in difficult circumstances, at a time when the northern port of Morocco was still occupied by Spanish forces, and a man had to show a passport at the Arbaoua border crossing. There were inevitable humiliations: the Guardia Civil searched all Moroccans, sometimes making them wait for hours before being processed, just to show them that they were no longer in their own country. Today, when he speaks of that displacement, he is inclined to use words like "absence" and "exile." As he sees it, his problems all began at that time. If he had remained in Fez, he wouldn't have lost all his friends or been made sick by this accursed East Wind. His exile is nothing less than a malediction. Well, perhaps that is an exaggeration. Life in this city has brought him a great deal of joy, even if he is inclined to forget this. For example, there was his good fortune in acquiring this house at a bargain price, and there were the excellent grades his children achieved in school. And there was the time when the *Paquet*, a steamer belonging to the Paquet Company, stopped on its trip to Marseille with its load of emigrants, allowing him to double his sales, since he was famous throughout Southern Morocco for the quality of his djellabas. But, today, when the air is so thin and he has such difficulty breathing, he is more apt to see things in a negative light.

Since he has located the source of all his ills, what is to be gained in summoning the doctor? His cure is dependent upon one thing alone: his leaving this city. That's what he'll do: he'll go to Fez, he'll go down to the medina and find the alley where he was born; he'll no longer lie here wallowing in nostalgia, keeping company with germs, with armies of organisms that move up and down his windpipe and come together in the night to strangle him. His asthma attacks are the result of a plot brewed by the demons of Tangier working in collusion with the East Wind, taking advantage of the absence, the disappearance, of his friends, profiting from his lack of sympathetic listeners.

If only he could go out into the garden and settle himself in a chair in the shade of the medlar tree. But all the chairs are broken. Not one of them will stand on its own legs now. They're all too old. Some have holes in them; others are missing their backs. If only he could spread a prayer mat on the ground and squat on it. Cross his legs and say his beads. Converse with God and his Prophet. Tell them about the wind and its misdeeds, the family and its betrayals. But they know all these things already; nothing happens to him that escapes their notice. So what is to be gained by complaining? Besides, it isn't necessary to go outdoors to do that. Leaving the house is out of the question. It's getting colder these days, and the garden is in an impossible state.

Slowly, his eyes makes a tour of the room. Everything is in its proper place; nothing has stirred. All the objects are immovable. It is from this fact that their spitefulness derives. There they sit, in their immobile arrogance, for all time. They will all outlive him. That heavy table fears neither the wind nor the cold; even attacked by damp, it shows no sign of weakness. That old radio, though it no longer works, will always occupy the same place on the shelf. That clock, repaired more than once, will sit there till the end of time, its hands fixed resolutely at twenty-two minutes past ten. It is on him that time works, not on the objects around him. Everything in the room seems to defy him: the drops of water on the windowpane, the worn carpet, the outdated calendar, the leather armchair whose springs have given way, the little table on which the teapot sits. . . .

Talking to himself again? Isn't that the first sign of senility? Talking to objects? Isn't that a sign of moral collapse? But he is neither senile nor morally bankrupt. He is old, that's all. No, not old; old age doesn't exist. It is an error, a misunderstanding between the body and the mind, between the body and time. It is a betrayal, a low blow that was prepared from the beginning of time, deriving its strength from the oversight of some and the violence of others, abetted by our own amnesia, our passionate attachment to roots and origins.

He must not talk to himself, he must put a stop to that. He will stifle the words as they try to escape his lips, he will keep a close watch on himself. He places one hand over his mouth, then smiles. The ability to laugh at oneself is a good sign. He has laughed so often at others, why not at himself? He makes no effort to stop. The hand over his mouth begins to shake. Between talking to oneself and laughing without reason, he prefers the latter, however absurd it may seem. But suddenly he catches himself muttering. He is unable to control the words that slip from his tongue. Now he is talking to himself *and* laughing! He must be losing his mind. Strangely, this thought does not alarm him.

He picks up an old newspaper, glances at it, tries to read a few words, then hurls it to the floor, cursing the years and their betrayal. Little by little, his eyes have abandoned him. He can see well enough to get around, but not to read. And he always enjoyed reading; he had a passion for works of history and old newspapers. His anger, as usual, is directed against one man in particular. He is convinced that if his eyesight is failing him, it's because a certain "louse" put the evil eye on him. He enjoys telling people about the time when he worked all day in his shop, cutting fine garments from bolts of white fabric. Passersby would stop to watch him, astonished and admiring, and would comment on his work. They were amazed at his dexterity, his rapidity, his skill. But the "louse," a hypocrite who spread bad luck in his wake, was jealous and placed the evil eye on him. And now, not only is he deprived of the pleasure of reading, but he can't even cut a straight line. His garments are no longer creations; they lack style and finesse. It's humiliating, cruel, intolerable. Oh, his solitude has become unbearably bitter. Life goes on without him, indifferent, beyond his sight, far from his reach. Unlike him, time does not crawl. In his irritation, he counts the hours, returning endlessly to the same objects, the same wall, the same dampness.

A bout of coughing, violent and convulsive, shakes him out of his reverie, momentarily upsetting the order of things around him. He knows that repetition of the same things over and over will lead eventually to madness. But he can't help it; it has become an obsession. He tells himself that he must not give way to it, that he must keep a grip on himself. He turns in circles, like a wounded beast, like a child on a leash. Again and again, he revives the balance sheet of his life. He relives his youth, the early days of the revolution in the Rif, the last political event that touched him. There is nothing wrong with his memory. It is only because he is so severe with himself that he allows himself to be scathing in his judgment of others. Is he malicious? Those who suffer the brunt of his sarcasm are inclined to think so. Indeed, there *is* something cruel about his irony. But why should he spare others? Why should he waste his time trying to understand them? Why should he make an effort to accept them? He would prefer to draw them into his web, to involve them in his gradual downfall. He can't help wishing people were more worthy, more intelligent, more fascinating and courageous, better than himself.

He gets to his feet, staggers, nearly falls, and

reaches out to seize his cane. He insults the door that doesn't close properly; he spits on the slippery tile floor, he curses the one he suspects of being the cause of his bronchitis; he complains to God about those who have failed to love him; he protests against all the immobile objects that surround him, sitting there in their quiet arrogance, enjoying their eternal well-being. A blue crystal vase, in particular, attracts his attention. He looks at it for a moment, then moves on, muttering: "It's older than I am. I'm younger than it. It has survived so much time, so much bad weather. It has emerged unscathed from so many journeys, so many moves. It will outlive me, just as it outlived my uncle who offered it to me as a wedding gift. But of what use is it? It has been placed there simply to defy me. It's intolerable!"

All it would take was a simple swipe of his cane to smash all these objects that cause him such irritation. But he restrains himself, more out of habit than avarice. He is aware of the malignancy of certain objects, but he is unwilling to confront them with their guilt. He is also aware of the danger of words. He manipulates them with great skill when he wants to hurt someone; he takes pride in using them that way. In that lies his strength. Words are his best companions. To be sure, they sometimes betray him, but they are also his support. As long as he is able to speak, as long as he is able to give birth to a violent outburst of invective, a hard, incisive assault to which there is no response, he will know that he is still alive, that his illness is only a temporary indisposition, a sinister shadow, a joke in bad taste.

He prefers words to be brief, subtle, full of nuance. He uses them with great finesse. He is famous for his words: they are arrows that wound, images that disturb, sounds that upset. He dreams of a house of words in which the syllables would be so tightly meshed they would form a long arabesque of light. This house would follow him from place to place. But he would stay outside it; he would not allow himself to live in it, for fear that he might become just another word, at the mercy of its own crazy syllables. The house would be a treasure trove from which he would be free to serve himself at will, at no risk to his security. At any given moment, all he would have to do was reach out and gather the words he needed. In fact, this house exists within himself. He knows this. And the knowledge causes him to laugh.

The doctor has dropped by to see him. He is a friend, a fine, generous man, patient by nature. He feels close to him. Fate allowed them to meet at a dramatic moment. The doctor's father was dying in Fez; here in Tangier, he found himself looking after a man who was not unlike his father, both having come from the old medina of Fez. Since then, an almost filial relationship has bound these two men to each other. Since they come from the same background, they share many similar memories. The same places, the same reference points, occupy their thoughts. The doctor is a young man, young enough to be his son. He knows how to communicate with his patient, never contradicting him, loving him with the feelings of a son who enjoys talking to his father. His care of the older man began by listening to him; he took the time to hear him out. They spoke of Fez, their birthplace; they compared their family trees. It's a wonder, really, that they didn't discover some second cousin in common.

To dispel the pain, to keep it at arm's length, it is often enough to talk, to gossip, to hold forth with a sympathetic companion. That's what life is. With the young doctor, he spends a great deal of time remembering life in the medina of Fez, evoking the quarter when it was inhabited by a number of large families. It troubles him to contemplate the current state of that city. He resents the sons of Fez who betrayed it by leaving it. As for himself, he had no choice. His partner decided to close their shop and open another business in Casablanca. At the time, he had neither the courage nor the means to follow him. So he chose the easiest solution: he came to join his brother in Tangier, where it was easier to make a living. This was when the city still enjoyed an international reputation. Tangier, in those days, sat at one of the world's crossroads, living on its myths and legends. He arrived just as its status was undergoing a change.

Far from allowing him to make his fortune, it left him with the bitterness of a missed opportunity. He had arrived too late. Today, it is this thought that obsesses him and causes him pain. He has never admitted the truth to himself, persisting in his belief that if he had come to Tangier a few years earlier, he would have made his fortune. What he fails to comprehend is that he was never the sort of man to make a fortune. He is a small-time merchant at heart, a tradesman who refuses to resort to slyness or subterfuge to make a sale. He always tells the buyer the truth, hiding nothing from him, not even his profit margin. He is a naive creature, a man of good faith. Obviously, these qualities are of little use in the world of business. This, he discovered to his own distress. Today, he can see that his good faith never made him any money. He doesn't regret it, but the thought continues to preoccupy him, especially when he compares himself with companions of his youth who also began with nothing but who now find themselves in possession of immense fortunes. He finds a certain pleasure in recalling that So-and-so, now the owner of a number of large stores, was once his apprentice, a mere delivery boy. . . .

The boxes of medicine are piling up on the dresser. Most of them have not even been opened. A few have torn wrappings, but the majority remain intact. What's the point of taking medicine if one isn't sick? From time to time, he swallows a spoonful of syrup to soothe his throat and ease his cough. In his eyes, medicine does not so much induce healing as oblige a man to face up to the fact that he is sick. He throws a box of suppositories into the trash can. He detests that sort of medicine. He never could stand it; as he sees it, such things are designed to humiliate a man. The doctor lacked a certain delicacy, a certain tact, in prescribing it. It is unthinkable that an old man should be made to insert one of those objects in his anus. There is something shameful in it, something degrading and offensive.

If the medicines are piling up, it is not because he continues to buy them, but because the doctor brings them to him. He thanks him graciously, as if the man had arrived with a bouquet of flowers. He sets them on a corner of the table, then, one by one, throws them into the trash can. He will have no visible signs of illness around him. Following an attack, he may swallow a pill or two to appease his conscience, though he's convinced they have no effect. He is proud of his ability to tackle his illness bare-handed. It's a direct confrontation, one to one, with no intermediary. Above all, he can't stand needles, not even when they're given by a beautiful young nurse. He prefers to imagine the nurse's hands gently stroking his body, helping him to forget his pain and his sadness. But that sort of thing isn't done—not in this house, at any rate. He dreams and smiles. He imagines himself elsewhere, in some other place at some other time. Soft hands caress his body. There is no one to interfere with his pleasure, no one to yell at him. He watches his doctor friend remove his white coat before accompanying him on a pilgrimage to the city of their birth. A white fog surrounds this picture. His eyesight must be betraying him again. He is still seated on his bed, facing the damp-streaked wall, listening to the sounds of the wind. He can not only hear the wind, but also see it. It is a human figure, with a smooth face and powerful shoulders. As it passes by, the sleeves of its burnous sweep over him, trailing wisps of cloud.

The wind. There is the enemy! It enters through the gap separating the southern tip of Andalusia and the northern tip of Africa. They call it the East Wind. It rises with the sun, but there is no fixed hour for its falling. When it reaches Tangier, it begins to move in circles, as if not knowing how to proceed. Rumor has it that if it arrives on a Friday, at the hour of noon prayers, the saints of the city will keep it there for seven days and seven nights. Some credit it with healing powers, claiming that it cleanses the city, driving away mosquitoes and microbes, carrying them off and dropping them into the sea. If the Strait of Gibraltar is polluted, it's because of the wretched East Wind, which deposits all those viruses in it.

But why must it attack the lungs of an old man? Why must it invade his house? It's so aggravating, especially when it begins to whistle and wail like an injured wolf or a mad dog. It blows hot, then cold; it slams unlatched doors; it hurls fistfuls of sand or dust in the faces of passersby; it causes migraines and upsets the nerves; it attacks old people. It is also the enemy of the fishermen, because when the sea becomes agitated under its merciless onslaught, the little fishing boats have to remain well anchored in a cove.

The wind is a natural force, but what about avarice? It is a way of life, a state of mind, a fixed vision of the world. A person is not born a miser; he becomes one. A man can put up with the wind and its havoc, but he is defenseless against avarice and its mean-nesses. Avarice and hypocrisy go hand in hand; they are more malevolent than any storm. He is fond of quoting the following lines from the Koran:

> *Alas for the acerbic calumniator,*
> *who, having amassed a fortune, spends his days*
> *counting and recounting it,*
> *who believes his fortune has rendered him im-*
> *mortal. . . .*

Or, if he wants to be more explicit, he will cite an-other verse from another section of the Koran:

> *Allah does not love those who are miserly,*
> *who embrace the doctrine of Avarice. . . .*

If he has no love for misers, neither has he any patience with those who squander their money. Here, too, he takes his authority from the sacred scriptures:

> *Squanderers are the brothers of the devil,*
> *and the devil is the enemy of the Lord.*

A great deal of his time is spent in drawing up lists of misers and spendthrifts. In his opinion, both are in the wrong because of their lack of moderation. Personally, he has always favored the middle way. And yet he has never practiced moderation in his speech. As one who has spent his life working his fingers to the bone but who has very little to show for it, he can only be resentful of those who have amassed riches and either hoard them or throw them away. This obsession with money is prompted by fear that he may find himself in need one day.

So he is tireless in his condemnation of the mediocrity of "the Devil's brothers," as he calls them, decrying their vanity and their superficiality. They embarrass and enrage him—as if it were *his* money they were spending! Most of the members of his family are inclined to be stingy, too, and how often he has wished they were a little more generous! But they are like the wind: there is nothing to be done about them.

Is he a misanthrope? Not really. He believes that

man is made to be good, just, humane. He knows it's a mistake, but he can't help having confidence in human nature. He likes those who appreciate his humor and who encourage him in his acerbic criticism. But he is so often disappointed. One by one, he has watched his illusions fall. He can't understand why his victims take offense and break with him. He tells himself it's because they are overly sensitive, because they lack a sense of humor. It doesn't seem to him that he is doing any harm in informing others of their weaknesses, their faults, their shortcomings. In his opinion the truth should always be told, even when it may be hurtful. So he goes on injuring; naively, clumsily, fiercely attacking others. And so, too, he always appears astonished by his victims' adverse reactions.

Now that illness has taken up residence in his body like a gaunt, ugly old woman; now that he must deal with it, even as he pretends to be unaware of its existence, he finds himself facing solitude in its most intolerable form. He is all alone with himself now, without a witness, without a victim. He is all alone in his bed, which has the imprint of his emaciated body, beside a table piled high with medicines, next to a water-stained wall that moves a little closer to him each day. He is afraid that, at any time, the four walls will close in on him and form a boxlike prison around him. He sees all too well what would follow. As in the days of the pharaohs, this room will become his tomb, a hermetically sealed cell, from which it will be impossible for him ever to escape. This picture causes a feeling of suffocation. He rears up with a yell, throws open the window, and takes a deep breath of cold air. This causes him to cough. He fills his mouth with water, swallows it the wrong way, and hurls the glass across the room. His wife comes running and supports him as she draws him back from the window. She places both hands against his chest in an attempt to calm the spasms that continue to shake his frail body. Once the seizure has passed, he collapses onto the bed with exhaustion. But he does managed to find the strength to make two or three acerbic remarks to his wife. She doesn't reply. Ordinarily, he can provoke an argument. But she merely squats on her prayer mat and turns her thoughts toward heaven. From the depths of his weariness, he begins to taunt her:

"Your prayers will never reach heaven, you know. They strike the ceiling and bounce back. It's because of all your prayers that there are so many cracks in this ceiling. Look, your prayers are all up there. . . . One good coat of paint, and they'd disappear. The roof of the house is collapsing with the nonsense you send skyward all day long. The heavier it gets, the less air there is in here. I feel as if I were suffocating. That's why the medicines do so little good. Their effect is annulled. So why would I continue taking them? I explained this to my friend the doctor.

Out of regard for you, he disagreed with me; he insisted that you have nothing to do with my troubles. But that's only because you've succeeded in recruiting him to your side. I'm all alone on my side. If I were to give up, there would be no one left to oppose you. . . . At any rate, I have dedicated myself permanently to solitude. I've never depended on anyone, I've always been on my own. Oh, I know that isn't something to brag about. If I tell you these things, it's simply so you won't forget them. I'm repeating myself, I know, but that can't be helped; you have to repeat yourself with women. . . .

"There now, she's gone. And I'm talking to myself again. That isn't good. It's very worrisome, in fact. I suppose I should spare her a little, but I can't bring myself to do it. I resent the poor woman. We've spent too many years together. It isn't even possible to say that we're growing old together. I'm growing old all alone. More precisely, we're growing old in the same house, each in a different corner. When I have an asthma attack, it's her duty as a wife to come to my aid, to give me something to drink, to help me until it's over. But I'm not obliged to thank her. She has never thanked me for anything. That's how it is. It's a question of education. They're taught to be suspicious of men. In most cases, this doesn't stop them from provoking their husbands and disagreeing with everything they say. It's their way of getting back at them. I remember the time a typhus epidemic struck

Fez. I was a child then. My father counted the coffins that passed by in the street. Almost all the funeral processions used our street, because it led directly to the cemetery gates. In the evening, he told us the figures: 102 dead, including 20 angels, 60 innocents, and 22 women! The women may not have been responsible for the typhus, but they had greater resistance to the virus than their menfolk. Of course, my father was exaggerating a little. He didn't like women; they had made him suffer. My four brothers all preceded their wives to the grave. I find that rather strange. It may be a coincidence, but I can't help concluding that they, each in her own way, precipitated their husbands' ends. That must be my wife's strategy, too. Of course, I wouldn't have the courage to accuse her of that. So I say it indirectly; I drop a hint here and there. I know that if my sons heard me speaking like this, there would be war. Each time they come to see us, they're taken in by the tears and the histrionics of my wife. That's why I'm all alone. There's no one to understand me, no one to defend me, no one to render me justice. On this sinister day, there is no one to talk to. So I hold my peace. I close my eyes so I can't see all the objects that lie around me, because everything in this house displeases me. I close my eyes and direct my attention elsewhere, into the past, to the time of my youth in Melilla, when I was a seductive, elegant twenty-year-old. In those days I would settle myself in the

Café Central, dressed like a British prince, with a monocle, and I would observe the lovely young Spanish women passing by, somewhat intimidated by their discreet glances. A woman's hand would graze my shoulder, and that would be enough to make me happy. I have always been fascinated by women: their bodies, their perfumes, their little wiles. I should have remained single, free. Then I would be able to spend my days on café terraces. I wouldn't be shut up in this damp room, confined to this sagging bed, face to face with this cracked wall and this woman who spends all her time praying, and surrounded by the ghosts of all my dead friends, who were carried off to heaven too soon, abandoning me to my loneliness and my stale memories, the pale, exhausted memories of events that may never have happened.

"Lola did exist. I still have her photo. But the women who caressed me with their eyes on the Café Central terrace—these were mere figments of my imagination. I am no longer an adolescent, who can believe in such fancies. I'm an old man, a wretched old man, whose lungs have been attacked by all the cigarettes he has smoked, by the East Wind, by the evil eye, by the presence of a wife who spends her days arguing with me. No doubt I am unjust in my evaluation of my wife. But I have to have someone on whom I can expend the energy that continues to keep me alive. It's strange, but I can't do without her. I'm upset when she decides to pay a brief visit to her daughter or son. But the moment she returns, I find myself growing irritated with her again. I tremble with fear when she falls ill, though I take care not to show it. I may stop taunting her for a while, but then I feel that something is lacking in my life. Between us there is more misunderstanding than tenderness. Anyway, I am suspicious of tenderness. It's a weakness, a snare, a form of hypocrisy that is alien to us. Tenderness, love, caresses . . . these things are not natural to us; they have been imported from the outside world. There is immodesty in such things.

"Is it possible that I am being extravagant—I who never stop grumbling and protesting, who am forever criticizing everything around me? Is it possible that I am being immoderate when, in the depths of my silence, I nurture the desire for a woman who may well be imaginary but who may also exist, who might be here at this moment to comfort me in my solitude, to caress my body and ease my pain, to help me forget my afflictions, my nervous disorders, my troubled sleep, my unjust rages?

"Well, that's how I am. I am ready to admit this to myself, but not to others. My severity with myself is a private thing; it's not something I'm about to shout from the rooftops. Perhaps that's why I find it intolerable when others judge me—the few who dare to do so, that is. But isn't that what they are doing by staying away from me, emphasizing my solitude with their absence, leaving me completely alone? Not one of my nephews has come to ask about my health. Oh, I can see them all come running on the day of my death. But I don't like to think of that. I'm superstitious. They'll be obliged to leave their places of business, to pass up a few deals, in order to put in an appearance at their old uncle's graveside, to pay their last respects. The day will be ruined for them. Meager vengeance! Petty revenge! The members of this family are more apt to put themselves out to attend a burial than a marriage. I've kept a list of all those who failed to show up for my elder son's wedding. I understand their motive. It's every bit as stupid as my rancor.

"What day is it, anyway? A sinister day. A day without sunshine or joy. Perhaps it's Friday. No matter. I must find the strength to go to Casablanca. I'm short on supplies. I have to be prepared for the holy day. Muslims like to dress in white on holy days. Yes, I must make the trip. Two hundred fifty miles, a whole day's trip! I could always place the order by telephone, but then some adulterous young man might take the opportunity to pass off some defective material on me. People are like that: if you put your trust in them, they cheat you!"

He is on the bus to Casablanca. An ancient vehicle, crammed with passengers, it advances hesitantly, stopping frequently to pick up more people. Tourists

generally enjoy this kind of trip: they find it pictur-
esque; it allows them to discover the country. They
bravely put up with the dust, the cigarette smoke,
the lack of toilet facilities, the noise, the wailing of
the beggars who climb aboard at each stop. It's not
a trip; it's a nightmare. He knows this, and yet he
tolerates it. The fact that he is able to undertake such
a journey at all is reassuring. He has defied his illness; he has snapped his fingers at those who tried
to prevent him from making the trip. He suffers in
silence, merely grumbling to himself, mocking the
vulgarity of his fellow passengers, but resolved to
act as if nothing has changed with the years, as if
his body is still a fountain of energy and youth. His
body is sound; it's his eyes that have suffered damage. He is not at all satisfied with what he sees and
hears. It is nostalgia that causes pain. He asks himself
why things must change, since people are always the
same, with their eternal smugness and air of self-
importance, satisfied with their certainty and their
mediocrity. To his astonishment, he loses his way in
the streets of Casablanca and is unable to locate the
faces and the landmarks he once knew. Each visit is
a trial. Sons have replaced their fathers in the business; he no longer recognizes anyone. This irritates
him. He lacks the courage to ask for news of this
one or that one, afraid of being informed of another
death. The lack of continuity, the repeated changes,
cause him great distress. As in the past, he examines

the merchandise, selects the best fabrics, places his order, haggles a little over the price, settles the bill, then goes on his way, relieved. He knows that they will try to cheat him, that some of them may even laugh at him behind his back. But he is no dupe. He conducts his business with the same rigor he exercised fifty years ago.

The merchandise arrives late and in a sorry state. Among the bolts of fabric, there is one that does not conform to his original choice. He doesn't put up with this sort of thing: he registers his protest by telephone and by mail, returns the defective material, and then waits for weeks for a response. This keeps him alert and lends him strength. It allows him to take revenge on the dishonesty of humans, on time itself. He is stronger than time. Time, in his eyes, is an old and formidable companion, a limping pirate, an empty sky, a white beach, a vacant lot filled with holes, a silent desert, a treacherous hand, a perfidious look. Ah, time! He often confuses it with the age in which he lives, an age of subterfuge, snares, and wicked laughter, with all of which he is intimately familiar. He has always made an effort to keep his mind alert, immune to the workings of time. His recollections of the past are all in their proper place, not a detail is missing. The facts are kept constantly within reach, ready at any moment to put in an appearance, faithful, precise, unchanged. Sometimes, he finds himself reviewing them—not because he's forgotten them, but because he's afraid he might. In this way, he tests his memory, he takes inventory, he evades the clutches of old age.

One of the sources of his pride is this fidelity to the past. It is also a source of regret, because he knows that he is in the process of becoming the last witness of an era. He looks around and discovers that he is all alone in the middle of a vast desert. There is no one else left; they're all dead or vanished. All gone, leaving only a few memories, a few images, the lingering echoes of a few faint voices. Straining his ears, he rejoices when he hears them more clearly. They are playing cards at a round table, drinking tea, laughing at everything and nothing. They must be somewhere nearby. This troubles him. It is *he* who is approaching them. The vision becomes clearer: they're beneath the earth, their flesh eaten by ants, their faces pared to the bone. They have no faces; only their teeth remain. Their voices continue to reach him, but they are more and more mixed together and indistinct. Perhaps that's what death is: familiar voices reaching our ears from beneath the earth, but distorted beyond recognition.

Objects are bad. In his opinion, they ought to be kept in a vault or a closed room, heaped together without order, as if they were worn out.

He throws nothing away, he keeps everything.

Objects that are of no further use are put in a store-room, where they fall victim to mold and rust. Evidence of a full life, they sit there for years in all their formidable uselessness. They are the signposts of a life, though they signify nothing precise: dead light bulbs, broken candles, old lamps, faucets, flat-irons, hundreds of keys of all sizes and shapes, radios, nails, balls of twine, chairs missing a back or a leg, shoes, tarnished mirrors, bundles of school notebooks, tattered bookbags, canes, a pair of gloves, even a dental plate. . . .

Though it has been some time since he lost his teeth, he has never had the patience to learn to eat with dentures. Rather than throw them out, however, he has stored them with all the other useless objects that tell the sad tale of his life.

He lives in horror of having to repair things that break down. He would prefer to stop a dripping faucet with a piece of string. He is no handyman. Still, he makes an effort to accommodate himself to those things that no longer work as they were meant to. When a piece of equipment shows signs of mal-functioning, he begins by ignoring it, hoping for a miracle; then he makes a few feeble attempts to get it working again—twisting pipes, turning buttons, tapping joints—finally, he curses the object soundly and renounces all further attempts to correct it. He had the spirit of a handyman but he lacks the knowl-edge. He detests all repairmen and journeymen—in particular, plumbers. He fails to understand why an object should suddenly stop functioning, any more than he can comprehend why cracks should appear in a wall or rust spots blossom on iron.

Between himself and the world of physical objects there has evolved a sort of perennial conflict. If objects are bad, he thinks, it is because they are durable, appearances notwithstanding. He observes them and says to himself: "How unjust! They will all outlive me. Functioning or not, they will go on sitting here, taking up valuable space, utterly indifferent to their uselessness!"

In the same way, he has a great deal of difficulty repairing the things that keep breaking down within himself. He refuses to admit that his body, which has endured so many hardships and survived so many battles, may one day betray him, may not respond with all the speed and agility that he continues to expect of it. Old age is the enemy, the void that takes up residence in the body and torments the mind. To accept it is to confess that one is vanquished, finished, it is to let oneself be carried off without a word of protest.

Obsessed with ideas of eternity, he has never been able to admit the real reason for his falling hair, his failing eyesight, his deteriorating hearing, his virus-infested lungs. With the same obstinacy, he refuses to understand why money should have lost so much of its value over the years. He never tires of telling people how he purchased his first house for fifty thousand centimes. That was in 1920, when a rial—twenty-five centimes—was enough to keep a family in food for an entire week.

The permanency of values, the immutability of things. He dislikes objects that move and alter the landscape, just as he dislikes movement and speed and people who are always in a rush. The years should be able to pass without kicking up such a fuss. Why must they leave their mark, their deep ruts, on faces, bodies, memories? This house alone is enough to testify to their passage. It is old and solid, certainly much older than he is. Built at the turn of the century by a Jewish family (he bought it from a Tangier rabbi), it is now in a state of extreme exhaustion. Besieged on all sides by dampness, it is in desperate need of repairs. In the past, no provision was made for heating houses, because Morocco always had the reputation of being a warm country. But for the last few decades, winters have been much harsher. Is it because the earth is growing colder, or is it simply because Moroccans have discovered the virtues of central heating? As for those virtues, not only does he fail to see them, but he adamantly refuses to introduce them into his dwelling. That is why the structure is invaded by damp and cold. He can see the cracks in the walls but he refuses to acknowledge their presence. He says, "They aren't cracks; they're simply discolorations in the paint."

To be sure, he has neither the courage nor the desire nor the strength to undertake repairs to the house. To do so would simply be to set a trap for himself. What is the point of making provisions for comfort that will only defy him, mock his lucidity, and scoff at his defenses?

"They're always wanting to repair something or other. You'd think someone had put them up to it. If I refuse to install central heating in the house, it's not for reasons of economy; it's because my body wouldn't tolerate the change. The moment I set foot outdoors, I'd catch cold. My lungs are fragile. My enemies don't consider such consequences; they simply want to be in style, to be modern. Well, their modernity is not for me. I'm a simple man. I don't care for appearances and I don't hold with waste. I belong to another era, perhaps to another civilization. It was a long time before I would agree to eat food cooked over gas. I'm an old-fashioned man; it's as simple as that. I'm the only one in this house to pay tribute to the merits of the past. It took me a long while to perceive the utility of a refrigerator, because I don't like things that are preserved artificially. The house suits me fine just as it is. I remember the day my children wanted to send me on a pilgrimage to Mecca. In the first place, I have always been repelled by those shoving, shuffling mobs. And besides, I preferred not to interfere with the picture I had created for myself of the holy places. Finally I understood that they were simply trying to get rid of me for a few weeks to undertake changes in the house. I thought: Never! As long as I'm still here, not a single plumber, not a single mason, will set foot in this place! They're all parasites, in collusion with time to destroy our cells!

"But why are they so resolved to undertake repairs to this house and its inhabitants? There's a leak in the bathroom. It's annoying, but does that mean we have to trouble a plumber? With a little patience, the hole can be plugged up. I could do it myself if my eyesight were better. And why doesn't that window shut properly? It's because the wood swelled during the summer. I keep it closed with the help of a big cushion. Nothing could be simpler. You can always come to an arrangement with things; you simply have to know how to go about it. The important thing is not to ill-treat them. That goes for me, too: I must not be ill-treated. For the moment, everything is in its place. I find this immobility a little disquieting. Well, I won't think about it anymore."

He dozes in silence that is punctuated by the ticking of the clock. The regularity of the sound irritates him. A hand of the clock leaps forward with each second. He raises his head, peers in the direction of the dresser, then, making a gesture of helplessness with one hand, gives up the effort. His age, his eventful past, his laborious trips, his tribulations, his accumulated trials—all these things serve today as a bill of health, a certificate of a full life. As he sees it, it authorizes him to give instructions to others. He believes that his experiences, coupled with his intelligence, should be put to the service of his fellow humans. But it is rare that anyone comes to him for advice. This troubles him. He is like a library that no one bothers to consult, a dusty collection of weighty tomes on history, moral philosophy, sociology, political science; a vision of the world and a philosophy that have great difficulty in making themselves known. He can't believe that it is because of his character that people take no interest in him.

"I want nothing but their welfare. What harm is there in wanting to share with others the fruits of my experience, the rewards of my trials, the substance of a life that began with the century? I know that most men prefer to turn to their wives for advice. Indeed, they feel obliged to do so. They are submissive creatures, who see women as their best counselors. Poor fools! If they submit to their wives, it's because they can't do otherwise. In this way, they hope to escape the fires of hell. That's normal. But can you see me discussing things with a woman, addressing her politely, listening to her opinions, weighing the pros and cons of a matter as if we were conducting a debate in the British Parliament? No! I can't remember ever having had an intelligent conversation with a woman. Right or wrong, my temperament always prevented it. My temperament is my best friend and ally. I have complete confidence in it. Those who consult their wives on every little matter have no temperament. My sons are a disappointment to me: not only do they never ask my opinion, but they follow to the letter the injunctions laid down by their wives. And when they want advice, they turn to their mother. They are in error on both scores. I don't know what I can compare them with. I can see that their wives are indifferent to me; there are moments when they are only a hair's breadth from showing me a lack of respect. I would like to have enjoyed friendlier relations with my children. That is the only area in which I must confess failure. They are much closer to their mother than to me. That's not surprising. I stand alone. No matter. I was always alone, and I was right to be so. I guess I'll just have to buy myself a bale of hay and keep it here at my side, so I'll have something to chomp on the next time someone decides to take me for an ass!"

This image affords him such pleasure that he repeats it several times, varying the statement with each repetition. One time the ass is a lamb; another time, a mule. The bale is composed now of hay, now of barley, now of straw. But through all this he remains the same old man, seated in the same place, tired of life, tired of himself, coming and going in a dark alley, raising his eyes periodically to gaze at the sky, glowering at the heavy clouds that are all in league against him on this interminable afternoon.

Doesn't he know that repetition is intolerable? Saying the same thing over and over in a variety of tones, in a stronger and stronger voice filled with rage, with an obstinacy and insistence that can make a deep and painful wound in anyone standing before him or cowering at his side. At times, the strength of his delivery may leave the impression that he is uttering a sentence for the first time, that his anger is prompted by the failure of others to accord him the attention he expects. His tyranny is inevitable. What he has to say lacks neither sense nor interest, but it loses both because it repeatedly has to bridge the gulf of misunderstanding that separates him from the rest of the world.

Possessing a memory that is in good shape, that can recall details with remarkable precision—when he talks of an event that happened sixty years ago, he can give the exact names of the persons involved, describe the setting in detail, and even recall the cost of certain articles that figure in the account—he never fails to silence all those who have the audacity to make sarcastic comments about his age. He takes pleasure in exhibiting a memory that has always made sure to deal in precise facts precisely recalled. No one can contradict him. In the family, he is looked upon as an infallible authority on matters regarding the past: births, marriages, deaths, feuds, divorces, important trips, snowfalls (two in fifty years), circumcisions, remarriages, bankruptcies, business deals, demonstrations against the French authorities. . . .

He has a large notebook in which everything has been recorded, including the price of the mint purchased on the day of a nephew's circumcision—a man who is now in his sixties!

In the days when the family still got together regularly, he used to enjoy reading aloud certain pages of this notebook. Nothing was concealed, neither the prices of goods purchased for a ceremony nor the most insignificant anecdote involving those who attended the event:

On this day, Friday, 1st Muharram of the year 1362 of the Hegira, a son was born to my brother Muhammad, by his second wife, Izza, a black woman. His white wife had packed up the children and taken them to visit her parents in Sefrou. Her brother had come to get them. The bus trip cost three rials. They took a jar of preserved meat with them. Before leaving the house, she locked the doors to the storeroom and the kitchen cupboards, and, of course, to her bedroom. Izza noticed all these things, but said nothing. The third wife, Dada, also black, rose from her sickbed to assist Izza and lend her moral support. The midwife was reluctant to come. In the evening, I went in search of her and had to pay her something in advance. It was a sad birth. My brother didn't realize what he had done. The boy was born at daybreak. He was black, like his mother. The baptism took place the following Friday. No member of the family was present.

I was ashamed. The sheep, purchased for 13 rials, was slaughtered with undue haste. The two slave women wept silently. Our other brothers came to the store of El Attarine to welcome the newborn. They said nothing indiscreet, but their wives made snide remarks. Forty days later, the first wife returned.

> *Written at Fez*
> *10 Muharram 1362 of the Hegira*

At this point, he would close the notebook and recount the remainder from memory. His concern was mainly the disputes that followed this event in the family history. He classified the various members under headings: indifferent, reticent, and malevolent. No one was spared. He gave a detailed account of the reactions and comments of each individual:

"You can never trust the offspring of slaves," Fatma said. Aicha added: "If this sort of thing is allowed to continue, we'll find ourselves being driven into the street." Khadouj said: "You can't trust them. You mark my words, that boy will avenge his mother one day." And Malika: "I thought blacks were hired to do the housework, not to have babies."

All these remarks are so many wounds to the vulnerable heart of the nephew, who is now a respectable civil servant. He still comes to the house from time to time to hear his uncle recount the circumstances of his birth. In order that the picture be complete, the older man sometimes colors his account with details about the political situation in Morocco at the time, listing the names of officers who had been dispatched from France to maintain order in a country in which the nationalist movement had begun to fester, especially in Fez.

As for the war, the Second World War, it was packed into a cardboard box that was closed and sealed. It contained a hundred or more copies of *Life*, as well as various other American magazines, all extolling the courage and the glory of the soldiers who landed on the beaches of Normandy. But when he left Fez for Tangier, he entrusted this precious carton to a relative, who forgot it, stored in a damp cellar, during a move. So a large part of his records was lost, leaving him unable to speak authoritatively about the war years, the details of which he knew only by hearsay; he had to rely upon the stories of poverty, near-famine, and Nazi atrocities that were revealed to the world following the German defeat. To this day, he remains convinced that Hitler had planned to eliminate Arabs once he had rid the world of Jews.

"As things stand, the rats in the medina of Fez know more about the Second World War than my imbecile of a cousin, with whom I stupidly left that box of historical records. Entrusting a treasure to such an ignoramus was like casting pearls to the chickens or feeding ginger to the mules. I am surrounded by ignorant people. If they upset me, it's because they don't realize how much harm they do. Some of them even have the nerve to put on airs, to parade their intolerable conceit. These, I have no choice but to disdain. I have nicknames for all of them. At first, people found it a little unseemly that I should mock my relatives in this way, but little by little the names stuck and became a form of identification. There is 'the consul,' a nephew who, to hear his mother tell it, was destined for a dazzling diplomatic career but who is reduced these days to selling djellabas to tourists. Then there is his obese, pasty-faced cousin, whom I have nicknamed 'the little white pot'; and there is 'the monster,' so called because of his raspy voice; and 'the rabbi,' a furtive, secretive creature; and 'the prior,' who spends a truly suspicious amount of time praying . . ."

The palm is reserved for his wife, for whom he has a whole catalogue of nicknames. In fact, he has never called the woman by her real name. The title he assigns her reflects the degree of disrespect he feels for her at any given moment. Sometimes, she is "the spider"; sometimes, "the "half-wife" (she is a small woman). One day, she is "the chatterbox"; the next, "the hurricane." These are all playful names. In moments of anger, she is more apt to become "the louse," "the lunatic," or something infinitely worse.

This mania for caricaturing others has brought him

a great deal of sorrow. He realizes this today. He is all alone. He has retained the esteem of almost no one. His words are like acid poured into open wounds; his statements have the power of a double-edged sword; his rancor is animated by an unfaltering memory and an inordinate pride. If he had gone into politics, he would have become an anarchist, a destroyer of illusions. But he has no love of politics and places no trust in the pronouncements of the politicians he hears on the radio and sees on television. He is a cultivated despot, who finds no one worthy of his esteem.

At the same time, he is not a bad man. Often, all it takes is a word or a gesture to bring out the goodness in him, to make him charming and cheerful. His ill-will is a superficial thing, the result of a fascination with words, a weakness for puns, many of which do not reflect his real thoughts. Words often get the better of him; they are inclined to betray him. But he sees no reason to complain about this. For him, they are words, no more, and people are wrong to react to them as if they were arrows or stones. He has always been fascinated with language, because it allows him to perform acrobatic stunts with his intelligence. When he cannot substantiate his opinions, even on some simple subject like fabrics or spices, he resorts to playing with words, often at the expense of others. If someone suggests that he is exaggerating, he will say that he must have got "the wrong spice." It delights him to be able to resort in this way to humor and irony. Though he will stop at nothing to protect himself from the attacks of others, he cannot understand why they grow angry with him when they find themselves the victims of his sarcastic remarks. He likes people. He is happy when his house is full of guests. As a sign of his joy, he switches on all the lights. It is hard to say whether his contentment derives from the fact that he has an audience for his jokes or that he is simply flattered by the presence of so many people in his house. If he is inclined to be acerbic with women, it is because he is inordinately fond of them. If he appears at times to be resentful of them, this is only because of his failure to seduce them all. On the other hand, he makes no bones about his feelings for children: he cannot stand them! He finds them irritating, ill-bred, spoiled, and sneaky. Their incessant noise gets on his nerves. No, he has no love for animals or children. He much prefers plants. He is capable of spending an entire day in his little garden, tending the trees and the flowers. There, he forgets himself, he dreams. This generally has the effect of calming his temper. Children are not gentle enough with him. They provoke him; they have no pity. Before the wedding of one of his nephews, he suggested that all the children be left at home. He was only joking, of course, but deep down he must have meant it. The groom, concerned for the safety of one dreadful brat, hired a baby-sitter to look after the child and to keep him out of harm's way during the festivities. How strange, an anarchist who dislikes disorder and fantasy! Nor has he any love of the superfluous, scorning all those things designed to enhance appearance and nurture vanity. All his life, he has searched for some simple object, some rare, indefinable object. This has been his secret passion. He has spent a great deal of time in antique shops and flea markets, stopping here and there to examine an object, considering it for a while, then moving on.

"One day I found what I was looking for. It was a superb Venetian mirror. A huge, heavy mirror, a little scarred in places. I fell in love with that mirror on sight. I decided I must have it, though I had no idea where I would hang it. It pleased me more than I can say. It must have been at least a hundred years old. At any rate, it was much older than I was. It made me so happy to rescue it, for it might have been bought by the owner of a brothel and been obliged to reflect things of a disgusting nature. What a fate for an object that must once have belonged to a great family, that must possess a wealth of glorious memories! Or it might have been broken by a violent gust of the East Wind. I saved it from such an ignoble fate. I hired a porter with a cart, and we crossed the city under the astonished eyes of the crowd. I came last, basking in the rays of light dancing over the surface of the mirror. Again and again people stopped to admire it, enchanted by the way the walls of the city and part of the sky were captured in this magic space. The images it gave back were strangely embellished, as if they had been reborn from the shadows in which they had lain for so many years.

"Since the day I installed the mirror in my house—and I'm the only one who was ever aware of its value—I have not stopped interrogating it. From time to time, it seems to me I catch a glimpse of a face in it, or a gloved hand, or a fog-enshrouded garden. I please myself by believing that it once belonged to a bewitching woman, someone like la Dame aux ca-mélias. The face that appears furtively in it is lovely but pale, with large, dark eyes, a beautiful head of hair, and a melancholy look. Perhaps it is a woman I once loved but never met. I often find myself think-ing of her: I invent her features, I dress her, I perfume her, and, like a foolish adolescent, I wait for her arrival. Of course, she never appears. She resembles no one I have ever known, not even Lola. It took me a long time, it took much patience and passionate desire, to catch so much as a glimpse of her face in the Venetian mirror.

"I am reminded of a girl with white skin and quick wit who came to the house one day to help with the chores. That girl troubled me deeply; I was awkward in her presence. She sensed this and took advantage of it to provoke me. I have a clear recollection of her small, tender breasts, pink and pointed, which moved freely beneath her loose blouse. They were visible whenever she bent over to serve me or to wash the floor. She was a real trollop. My wife almost went out of her mind with her. The girl had all the advantages of youth, a pretty face, a body impatient to be caressed, and far more insolence than was good for her. Finally, my wife dismissed her. She left the house in tears. Later, she telephoned me two or three times at the store. I was panic-stricken. But there are moments, even today, when I miss her. What a trial that was! I was certain I would lose control of myself. Folly had brutally infiltrated our house. One day she had the nerve to tell the neighbors that the old man didn't have long to live, that she was going to reorganize his life from top to bottom. That sort of thing is not uncommon in our country. I felt like a character in one of those interminable Egyptian serials. She had decided to live out some story she had seen on television. TV was the extent of her culture, her major point of reference, the source of all her dreams. Ah, she was lovely. But she did well to leave. I preferred it that way. Then I could imagine her as I wished, I could do as I liked with her image, her silhouette, her irritating laugh, her curious habit of tossing her hair now to the front of her head and now to the back. . . .

"My hands are trembling. It must be the cold. My hands have aged terribly. Hands are a clearer indication of age than the face. I try to imagine these tired hands moving over the soft, warm thighs of that girl. I never succeeded in obtaining the least caress from her. And yet her eyes, her movements promised so much. . . . But I'm not an old fool, obsessed with beauty and the need for caresses. People imagine that desire is extinguished with age, but they're wrong. Desire not only remains alive, but also grows. It may be a little less insistent, but it's there, all the same, setting the skin afire, creeping up to torment you in the night. I refuse to lie down and die. There are times when I am unable to control my gestures. All by themselves, my hands come to rest on a woman's shoulders, in the hope of grazing a breast. People don't understand. Even if it becomes unbearable, I'm not going to begin praying that the fire of my desire be extinguished. There's nothing wrong in allowing oneself to be moved by desire, not even at my age. It's a sign that there's still life in the body. That's how it is. I can do nothing about it. Is it my fault that girl burned with desire, that her firm, young body stimulated me by its presence? In whom can I confide? To whom can I tell all these things? If only Touizi were here! He would understand."

The address book sits on the little table. It is a blue school exercise book, about nine inches by seven. In the house, it is known as "the Joan of Arc," because on the cover is a drawing of Joan on her horse, her sword held proudly aloft. In the lower left-hand corner, in small letters, is the trade name: MAPAMA. On the back cover are four tables, for addition, multiplication, subtraction, division. Between Joan's head and her sword, the following words have been written: "This book contains the telephone numbers of family, friends, and neighbors."

He picks up the book, flips through it, sets it down. Then he seizes it again and opens it at random.

Hadj Muhammad, Melilla: 32.14 (store); 32.51 (home). Abdelaziz, his son (officer): barracks tel: 31.01. Otman, his youngest son (unemployed): no telephone.

They're all dead. The man buried his wife and his children, then faded away from sadness and neglect. He was an aristocrat who squandered his fortune on loose living, travel, and gifts. At the end of his life, he found himself destitute, with not enough money to pay the doctor. But he was a good man. More than a cousin, he was a friend. Remembering him, he feels tears welling in his eyes. He turns the page, not wanting to give way to his sorrow. He comes upon *Doctor Murillo: 342 51, Tangier*. This man saved his life twenty years ago when he was suffering from pneumonia. He, too, met a sudden end. When he learned of his death, he wept. He was really afraid; the doctor was the only person he trusted. A Spaniard, he had taken up residence in Tangier from love of the city, and enjoyed a reputation second to none. His death was felt by the people as a great loss. For a long time afterward, he refused to see another doctor.

He flips through the pages in the hope of coming upon the name of some sympathetic soul who might still be alive. Dhaoui, the cripple. He's still around, but he's a bastard. He has been an informer for both the Spanish and the French police. Since the granting of independence, he's been a *mokadem*, a sort of unofficial agent who knows everything about everyone in his quarter. His number is in the book because his services were once required, when a street gang threw stones at the house. The man proved useful at the time, though he exacted a steep price for his services: for years, he obtained his clothing at the store for nothing.

Some pages contain nothing but scribbling—the children must have got their hands on the book. Then he comes upon the name Daoudi, an old friend who loves Andalusian music. Not only is he alive, but also he is well. He may be out of town, though; he spends a great deal of time on the road, following the National Orchestra of Andalusian Music on its tours. He has the telephone brought to his bedside, dials the number, and waits. A woman's voice answers. Wrong number. He dials again, more carefully this time. The line is busy. He smiles. He is reassured. On the third try, he has Daoudi on the line. What a relief! In order to bring the man running, he concocts a lie:

"My son has just sent me a tape of Hadj Abd-el-

Krim Raïs's orchestra. It's one of his best. I'd like to play it for you. It's a concert he gave in France, with a number of ministers and ambassadors present."

Daoudi, who has a private income, is a cultivated man, jovial and generous. He arrives with a tape player and a little case full of tapes.

"How are you feeling?"

"I'd be a lot better if I could go outside. But with this wind and rain, who can go anywhere? Just seeing you does me good, though."

"So it goes, my friend. There are those who win and those who lose."

"What have you been doing lately? Still up to your neck in music?"

"More and more! But Raïs is sick at the moment, so his orchestra isn't doing much these days."

"Tell me, what do you think of the way they've introduced the piano, the saxophone, and another guitar in this music?"

"Terrible! It's disgusting! It's heresy, I tell you! What a nightmare! Five centuries of tradition thrown out the window to make way for these . . . instruments! The piano, I can stomach, but the rest—it's a scandal! . . . But, tell me, how are you doing?"

"Fine, I'm fine. A little lonely, but otherwise not bad. I cough, I choke, I'm bored with myself, but I'm doing fine. . . ."

"Did you hear about Hadj Omar?"

"The one who's rolling in money?"

"If you like. The brother of Moulay Ahmed. You know, the bald fellow they call 'the little cheese' because of his pasty complexion."

"What happened to him? Did he die?"

"No, no. He's remarried. When his wife died last year, he didn't waste any time in tracking down a replacement. His children got together and offered him a choice: remarriage in exchange for renouncing his fortune. Can you believe it? He agreed! He sacrificed everything: house, business, possessions, in order not to have to sleep alone."

"And he was right! But his children should be ashamed of themselves. They could have let him remarry without depriving him of all his possessions. After all, if they're rich, it's thanks to him."

"Yes, but you know how young people are—they have no pity. On the day of his death, the new wife won't inherit a cent."

"But that's illegal!"

"Of course, but there are ways around these things. He signed every document they stuck under his nose. At any rate, he won't be able to take his fortune with him."

"So Hadj Omar has remarried! What's she like?"

"Young, very young. A schoolteacher. An orphan."

"Do you suppose he can still . . . ?"

"And you, can you still . . . ?"

"Of course. That's my problem! I still can, but with

whom? From time to time, I talk about taking a new wife, mainly to sound out the others, but without any real conviction. When a man reaches my age, people think he's finished. . . . So, Hadj Omar is happy?"

"He looks younger than ever."

"Of course, that's all it takes to rejuvenate a man."

"These are not good times we're living in, my friend. There's so little respect among the young. Of course, there's no work for them. But frankly, they don't have much ambition. And nothing is done to help them. Have you seen the state of the hospitals? Those who can afford it go to France to be treated. Some even go as far as America! Well, we won't talk about that; it's much too depressing. Tell me, how is your health?"

"Oh, I'm not too strong. People go out of their way to irritate me. That starts me coughing and gasping for breath. I'm not sick; I simply have to put up with all these idiots. But I'm glad to see you. I was a little afraid to call you. And what about you? Have you remarried? I mean, have you taken a second wife?"

"My second wife is music. It's become my *raison de vivre*. You can't imagine the satisfaction it brings me."

"Andalusian music makes me sad. It reminds me of all the festive occasions in my life that will never return. For some reason, I've always associated that music with these special occasions. It makes me nostalgic. And I don't like nostalgia. . . . How about your children? Are they doing well?"

"They're all grown up now. Their mother and I live alone in the big house. I've installed central heating. Unlike you, I'm not afraid of comfort."

"Well, I'm not a wealthy man, you know. . . . Think of it! Hadj Omar was once an apprentice in my fabric shop in Fez. I taught him the trade. He left for Casa, and I, like an idiot, came to Tangier to contemplate the sea and let myself be whipped about by the East Wind. It was a stupid move on my part!"

Daoudi places a cassette of Andalusian music in the player. They sip their tea. He keeps time to the music with his right hand. His friend dozes off. He's sleeping now, dreaming of all those who have made their fortune and who have had the good luck to remarry.

The blue address book sits on the table. It's a simple matter of opening it at random to evoke a memory, a ghost, a man still miraculously among the living.

The drip-drip of the leaky faucet can no longer be heard. It hasn't been repaired; the water has simply been shut off. The walls are still standing, despite the humidity and the cold. The plaster on the false ceiling has begun to crumble in places, there are a few holes here and there, but the roof is still intact.

The refrigerator, an American contraption, is no

longer functioning properly. It's very old—impossible to know how old exactly. It was bought second hand, but it must have served several families, several generations. The motor makes a strange noise. And it no longer keeps things cool. They'll have to start keeping their food outdoors. It's cold enough out there. How many tons of provisions did that refrigerator hold in its lifetime? How many gallons of water did it chill? This isn't the first time it has broken down, but this time it must be for good. He can see it through the half-open door. He can hear it. The motor is about to give out. No more cooling, no more ice-making. It's tired; it's old. It's dead.

Life in the house won't be the same following this most recent breakdown. No repairmen will come and look at such an old machine. They are all familiar with the refrigerator, they all know it for the rare, useless object it is. Well, they'll simply have to make do without it. Of course, there's no question of thowing it out. It can always serve as a cupboard, to hold dishes or fruit. And then it will be necessary to find a replacement. There's always the second-hand market. But that will mean shopping around, bargaining. The only alternative is to buy a new one. But locally made refrigerators are of notoriously poor quality. They are thrown together any which way; they are not designed to last. Some people still manage to get their hands on imported models. Foreign manufacturers are inclined to take their work more seriously, so their products are generally of higher quality. This is not blind prejudice; it is a well-documented fact. It's the same with everything. Think of the number of people who prefer to go outside the country for medical care, though that costs money. He has no intention of going outside the country himself, and he doesn't hesitate to criticize those who do. The state of the hospitals in Morocco is deplorable—everyone knows that. Some fifteen years ago, he had to be hospitalized. The memory of the experience is very disagreeable. The doctors and nurses were attentive enough to his needs, but he couldn't close his eyes to all the filth, the negligence, the lack of seriousness in the place. It was the unsanitary conditions that troubled him most.

If he has no intention of going outside the country for medical care, it's because he isn't sick. Besides, he's afraid of airplanes. And he doesn't have the means to treat himself to such luxury.

Right now, his resentment is directed against the American who built that refrigerator. If *he* manages to keep going, in spite of everything, why should the objects all around him persist in breaking down, as if they were endowed with souls?

"That's it," he says. "The refrigerator has given up the ghost simply to defy me, to add to my troubles. It's intolerable! Everything happens at once!"

Though it is not his intention to compare himself with the malfunctioning refrigerator, the leaking faucets, and the house that is growing old, he understands that there exists a bond between himself and these objects. He cannot tolerate wear, whether in objects or in men. The batteries in the transistor radio annoy him when they wear out, so he always takes his time to replace them. Just as he is reluctant to admit that his eyesight is failing, that his hearing is not as good as it once was, and that his friends are all disappearing, he refuses adamantly to accept the fact that things eventually wear out and become useless. Only the superb Venetian mirror, even if it has lost a little of its sparkle, does not turn his certainties and obsessions upside down. He still finds pleasure in looking at himself in it. It hangs in the hallway, where it occupies itself in reflecting selective images. He likes to remember how he fell madly in love with it the day he found it sitting on the sidewalk. He gazed into it for a long while, imagining that he could detect all the images that had been stored up in it for decades. It amused him to identify himself in a mirror that had had such a long life and that must contain a wealth of extravagant and intimate memories. It probably once belonged to a great family, foreigners, no doubt, who had lived in Tangier when the city still had an international reputation. Like most Europeans, they had probably left possessions behind when they went back to their own country, one trace of their passage being this solitary treasure, this glass-and-plaster relic of their brief sojourn in the city. All a person would have to do was stand before it and interrogate it in order to learn one or more of its secrets. Such a large, clumsy object was not something that could easily be carried around. Moving it would be as risky as leaving it sitting out on the sidewalk, where anyone might come along and abscond with it.

Now, the mirror is here, hanging in his house, a house that has lapsed into silence. He rises and approaches it. Is he about to add to its burden by imposing on it the entire weight of his lassitude and his solitude? Or is he about to engage it as a witness, a friend, an accomplice, at this difficult moment in his life, when the whole world is in league against him?

He gazes at it, admiring its beauty, though he sees nothing in it. It is a piece of sculpture, no more, a purely gratuitous, useless work of art.

"Ah, if only it had the power to carry off certain indomitable enemies! It would be so simple: all you would have to do was stand someone before it for a moment or two, just long enough for the person to be painlessly absorbed. Then it would be a precious object! I can see the crowds now, filling the alley outside the house, each with an enemy in tow. I could make a fortune. Guaranteed disappearance! Not a trace left! If I could stand a certain man before this mirror, a man I hate with all my heart, a man I haven't ceased cursing for the past thirty years, then

I would be happy. I have a number of names for that man: the heartless one, the traitor, the supreme hypocrite, the sniveling upstart, the scorched pot, the miser, the supreme egoist, the breaker of vows, the plague. . . . If only I could take my revenge on him, turn back time and correct history, erase a certain gesture of confidence and generosity on my part, and leave him with nothing, just as he was before I met him. Ah, the liar, the moon-faced creature, the mortal embodiment of evil and treachery!

"The story is simple. It involves a man I took into my house and treated like a son. My own sons were still children when he came on the scene, his hands empty, his eyes filled with intelligence and ambition. I said to myself: 'This is exactly the man I need, the son I would like to have.' In those difficult times, when business was so bad in Fez, merchants were abandoning the city, taking themselves off to make their fortune in Casablanca. I did not have the courage to follow their example. When the young man arrived on my doorstep, I had made up my mind to go to Tangier to join my brother, who was doing a lucrative business. With his profits, he had opened a number of shops. Each of his sons had his own store. Business was flourishing. Finally, I liquidated my assets in Fez and headed for Tangier. But I didn't receive the sort of welcome I had expected. How can I ever forget the embarrassed look in my brother's eyes as he informed me that I'd come at a bad time, that he could do nothing to help me, that everything was in the hands of his sons? This was the second blow to my pride—the first being my separation from my city. I turned to my nephews for the names of suppliers and for advice on how to get started. That, too, was a mistake. Their idea of morality was every man for himself. Oh, that *was* a difficult time! But somehow or other I managed, with the help of neighbors, Jewish merchants I didn't know. It was in the Jewish community that I found the goodness and generosity I failed to find in my own family. I have always had good relations with Jews, both here and in Melilla, Nador, and Fez. We come from different backgrounds, we practice different religions, but we've always been willing to lend one another a hand. I was excluded by my nephews. My rancor, my disappointment, my rage, all date from that time. I sent for the one I had come to look upon as a son. I took him out of the medina of Fez, where the last businesses had closed. I took him into my home. For all intents and purposes, my wife became his mother. He had lost his own father at a very young age. I took care of him, without any thought of recompense. I introduced him to my brother, my nephews, my nieces; I even arranged his marriage, with an unmarried niece. I did everything a father should do for his son. I spent my savings to ensure his comfort and his happiness, hoping in this way to keep him at my side, hoping he might show his gratitude

someday by going into partnership with me, by helping me to turn my shop into one of the most suc-
cessful in the city. I was getting older, I had to slow
down, so I placed all my hopes in that young man.
I relied on his assistance and his support. I wanted,
this time, to be a success, especially because earlier
everything I had undertaken had failed. And what
did the traitor do? He abandoned me! He preferred
to offer his intelligence and his energy to my nephews, my competitors, my adversaries! Since then,
things have gone steadily downhill for me. I'm not
exaggerating. And my life is a failure because it is
undermined by hatred. My wound has become a
canyon, through which flows a river of hatred. Thirty
years later I still can't bring myself to forgive this
man for his betrayal. I want only justice. Such a little
thing! Yet it is the impossible I demand: a return to
the past, a repayment of the debt, material and
moral. It makes no difference; it must be repaid. I
alone continue to demand reparation, however. His
"mother" defends him. She prefers to take the side
of her "son" against her husband. That's normal.
But why should I respect a woman who betrays me
in her turn? Why should I be merciful and patient
with those who have done me wrong? There are
times when I find myself alone in this house, when
my wife is away on a visit to her daughter in Fez or
her son in Casablanca, times when I'm obliged to eat
alone, to reheat the same dish over and over for the

entire length of her absence. And do you think the traitor ever makes a move in my direction? No, he prefers to abandon me to my cold solitude. What am I supposed to do? It's a disgrace. Once, I went so far as to enter his shop and tell him exactly what I thought of him, his wife, and his children. But I wept bitter tears the day his eldest daughter died. Poor girl, only eighteen years old; she didn't deserve to die. I felt pity. I wept. At the same time, I was ashamed of my feelings. It would have taken so little—a gesture, a word, a sign of affection—to wipe out the score inscribed in the bottom of my heart, to wipe it out forever, as on the Day of Judgment. But pride is an unreliable counselor. There were a few attempts at reconciliation, but they were superficial. Our hearts remained closed, impenetrable; the rancor festering there remained ineradicable. When a man has been betrayed and humiliated as I have, the resentment remains for life. I'm not sick; my lungs are a little congested, that's all. But I have been deeply wounded. Few people understand me. They tell me these things are all in the past, that I must put them behind me, that life goes on, that things change. How can I learn to forgive? I know of no way to forgive and forget. Ah, if only there were a village where the morning breeze had the power to induce forgetfulness, to make forgiveness possible, easy. Not only will I never forgive that man, but my aversion for him extends to everything that touches him. I can't abide his wife or his children or his friends. I know I'm wrong, but the feeling is stronger than I am. It's impossible for me to play the hypocrite. I feel that if I were to be reconciled with him, I would lose a great deal of my strength. I have placed myself in an inextricable situation, I know. I need the man to survive; I am dependent on his errors, his betrayals, his very existence. I must be grateful to him for having become such an obsession, for having ruined the last thirty years of my life. Yet, he has filled them to the brim. Perhaps, it is for this reason that I felt compassion when his daughter died. I wept because our enmity is one of the things that binds us. I am not a monster; I am incapable of doing harm to anyone. I repeat this to all those who suspect me of being malicious. I am simply dissatisfied with things as they stand. For a long while, I waited hopefully for something that never came. That is why I grumble and growl, that is why I grow irritated, that is why I give free rein to my surliness and arm myself with words. But the words are ineffectual, the words are empty and lack substance. All they do is calm me momentarily, give me the fleeting impression that I have settled the score. But since they have no magic power, I am obliged to repeat them. And so it goes, year after year after year.

"Poor me! Reduced to repeating the same words over and over, succumbing to the same impotent rage. Reduced to returning ceaselessly, meticulously, to the words I uttered the day I learned of his betrayal. If I rant and rave, it's not because I'm growing old. No; my problem is that I am a young man in an old man's body. Age has nothing to do with it. I'm angry because I have been refused justice, I'm frustrated because I have been swindled. And not for anything in the world will I renounce my passion. I am marking time now. Nothing moves, but everything is falling apart. My feet are tired. I have corns on the soles of my feet, between my toes, on my heels; they're hard and they hurt when I walk. I've been dragging them around with me for years now. They date from the time of the great betrayal. I've grown thin; I have hardly any flesh on my body. My bones are visible, and my back is stooped. It comes from the weight of the world's stupidity resting on my shoulders. My hands are big and strong—they haven't changed. It seems to me I have nice-looking hands, though no one has ever remarked on them. But it's true; my hands alone have remained youthful and attractive. In this country, people pay no attention to hands. Yet a woman who has ugly hands, even though her face is pretty, is a woman who is missing something. Men are more inclined to take an interest in a woman's legs, but in this country, the djellaba conceals (or used to conceal, since today they wear skirts and jeans) those essential parts of the body.

"I don't like small women. My wife is rather small

83

in stature. I often tease her about that. She takes this badly, and that amuses me. But no one is amused when I begin to denounce her traitor of a son. All our disputes turn on his action. She never fails to come to his defense, and I simply cannot understand how she can defend a traitor, one who abused my confidence and my generosity.

"But I must stop this. I can feel anger rising within me. What I find curious is that my rage is still alive after all these years, that I never tire of it. There are days, like today, when I grow tired of myself, but I never tire of the rage that washes over me every time I think of that man. I know everything about him; nothing escapes my attention. I can calculate almost exactly the size of his fortune; I know about all his projects, his ambitions; I know what he eats, who his friends and his enemies are. Sometimes, it seems that he interests me more than my own sons. Perhaps that's why I'm so resentful of him. Our enmity is known to everyone. Few take my side. That's as usual. I'm all alone on my side. Those who speak ill of him in my presence are hypocrites; they just say what they think I want to hear. At the same time, I don't like to hear people abusing him; no one has any right to do that. On the surface, the man is kindness itself; he is affable and obliging. I have often seen him with others: he's polite and sociable, a cultivated man. It is for these qualities, and his intelligence and vivacity, that I once looked upon him as a potential partner and treated him like a son. But he preferred to involve himself with scorpions and vipers. I know that he has suffered, but that is not enough to appease my anger. It seems to me that my rancor helps to keep me alive. Let him come and express his regrets, let him come and present his excuses, let him come with his hands clasped behind his back and his head lowered, let him kiss my hands and ask my forgiveness—then we'll see. I'll weep on that day, I know; I won't be able to restrain my tears.

"I'll never forget the day when, during a baptism luncheon at the home of one of my nephews, a young churl treated me with disrespect because of an open window. I wanted it open so I could breathe more easily, but the young man wanted it closed. When I opened it, exercising my authority as the elder, he shoved me roughly aside and slammed the window shut. My feelings were hurt. I turned, with tears in my eyes, and left the house. The traitor followed me into the street and led me back inside, where the young man muttered his apologies. I appreciated the traitor's gesture. For once, he had acted like a son."

It's time to switch on the television. He summons the cleaning woman and points in the direction of the set with his cane. Someone is singing—or, rather, lamenting. The puffy face is framed by sand dunes. The singer's eyes are glazed. In the background is a straggly palm tree. The whole scene is artificial and boring. The pages of a small book flutter.

He waits for the cleaning woman to leave the room before delivering the following comment: "She drags her backside around the house all day, and he spends his time massacring the language of Chawqi!" As he sees it, there is something terribly wrong with the world. But what possible relationship can there be between the exhausted body of a poor woman who has been in his service for years and the voice of a blind man bewailing his wretched fate in the desert? He invents a relationship: if it were a lovely, luscious young woman who had come to switch on the TV set, he would not have to listen to the tired intonations of a blind man, but would find himself basking in sweet strains of ethereal music.

He respects religion but he is afraid of temptation. He often thinks of hell: he sees it, he smells it, he believes in its existence. It is a place of fire and blood; he knows that. It strikes him that a thought he entertained a moment ago was improper. He has committed a sin. Not a very serious one, to be sure, but he would prefer not to repeat it. He rises, seizes the little black stone he uses in his ablutions, squats on the carpet, and begins to pray. He asks forgiveness of God. He prostrates himself and appeals to the prophet Muhammad. He apologizes for allowing such confusion to reign in his soul. Why do such contradictory ideas, thoughts that normally would cancel one another out, take shape simultaneously in his brain? Is it a sign of fatigue, old age, senility?

With one hand, he brushes away such an unseemly idea. Then he smiles, because he knows it will take more than this simple gesture to banish such thoughts. For a few moments, he imagines a host of young women passing before him, each removing an article of clothing. He revels in the little spectacle he has staged for himself on this sad afternoon.

"What harm can there be in that?" he asks himself. "I'm only imagining these things. No one, absolutely no one, can prevent me from imagining what I choose to imagine. My passion is not alcohol or cards; it is women. Besides, I am in possession of distressing widsom. If I'm wise, it can't be otherwise. From time to time, my hand steals a few furtive caresses from the anonymous bodies that float about me. That's shameful, I know, but what is even more shameful is to deprive an old man of female companionship. Ah, if only I had a girlfriend! She would come to keep me company. I would tell her funny stories; I would make her laugh. And she would let me hold her hands. What harm is there in that? Alas, there's no way to realize such a thing. So I must live with my fantasies. I can't help it if there is sometimes a collision between what is permitted and what is not. May God forgive me! At any rate, He alone has control over what goes on in my head."

The telephone rings, causing him to start. He has never grown used to this sound, nor has he succeeded in lowering the volume. It's a wrong number.

A woman's voice has asked for Moulay Ahmed. He informs her that, in his house, no one is addressed as Moulay, especially not Ahmed, the car watchman who comes from time to time to join them for dinner. Moulay is a sign of superiority, nobility, a sign of aristocratic birth. He has never approved of people putting on airs that way. He doesn't like the telephone, even less since his hearing began to fail. He asks the caller to repeat herself. Then, still failing to understand, he hurls the instrument to the floor. It has been placed here deliberately to remind him that he is losing his hearing, just as the television set has been left here to point up the fact that he is losing his eyesight.

Ahmed no longer stops by the house for something to eat. It's just as well; he suspects the man of wanting to seduce his wife. He's a young fellow, barely out of his twenties, and rather good looking, with bright eyes and thick curly hair. He knows his wife is partial to curly hair, since she has often expressed her regret that her sons have such stiff, straight hair. He has forbidden Ahmed to come unannounced to the house. The last time that happened, he made a frightful scene. His wife was shocked. At the same time, he thought she was a little flattered to learn that she was still capable of provoking his jealousy. Yet there had been nothing ambiguous in her behavior. She had fed Ahmed in the kitchen and asked him for news of his wife and children, who were visiting their grandparents in the country. But that little exchange was enough to provoke the terrible scene, which was interrupted at one point by a fit of coughing. His wife still cannot make up her mind whether he is jealous or is simply trying to annoy her. She'll never forget how, in the early years of their marriage, he always kept the front door locked. She was allowed out only once a week, to go to the hammam; and even then he insisted on accompanying her and went to get her in the evening. Once or twice, he forgot the time and could be seen hurrying toward the hammam, muttering under his breath. Jealousy was a part of the tradition; it was in the order of things. But what does it mean to be jealous at his age? He is over eighty, and she is in her early seventies. So it isn't a question of age. For her, it is a form of lunacy; for him, a question of habit and tradition.

He can't remember the last time they slept together as husband and wife. He would prefer not to think about that. It must be at least fifteen years since they started sleeping separately, though they continue to occupy the same bedroom. There are many empty rooms in the house, but they have decided to remain together. Each knows that the reason for this is fear. Fear of everything and nothing. Fear of dying alone. Fear of being attacked by robbers. Fear of being visited in the night by a ghost. Fear of awakening to discover that the other has died during the night.

They admit this fear but push it to the back of their minds, not wanting to think about it. In any case, they never discuss it, despite the chronic animosity that rules their relationship. Neither can find it in his heart to rejoice over the gradual collapse of the other's health. From a distance, it might almost seem that there was more weariness than tenderness in their marriage. But actually he has never made a display of his tenderness. In his eyes, that sort of thing is a weakness, except when it's directed toward children. He doesn't say "I love you," but "Why don't you love me?" He weeps with emotion each time one of his children leaves after a visit. He tries to conceal his tears, but he rarely succeeds in doing so.

Daoudi has gone, leaving a cassette of Andalusian music in the tape player. It is dark. He will have to get up and switch on the lamps. His wife is asleep; he can see her stretched out on a mattress in the living room. He calls her—not by her real name, but by one of her innumerable nicknames. She doesn't answer. Perhaps she is really asleep. Or perhaps she has died in her sleep. This thought frightens him. He rises with difficulty and goes to check on her breathing. He is relieved. She's only asleep. He mutters a few disparaging remarks. She has frightened him. That isn't good. It doesn't seem to him that she has the right to cause such an emotion in him. Tenderness, in his case, appears ill-natured; it lies buried within him and it causes him pain. He switches on the lamp. He would like a glass of hot tea, but he doesn't want to ask for it. He knows that the request will come out in an aggressive tone. He is annoyed that she is sleeping just when he needs her to prepare his tea. He might wake her gently, but he can't bring himself to do it. It's stronger than he is. He has never been gentle with her, so he doesn't see how he could start to be now. She wouldn't understand. It would be a mistake.

Late afternoons in winter are like rocky roads, long and uncertain. It is so easy to lose one's way on them. And there is always the danger of some strange, alarming encounter. Hands emerge from the fog or from behind a tree to beckon toward the shadows. Bushes change location without warning, carrying everything else with them.

Late afternoons are interminable. It is perhaps for this reason that he grows drowsy and now and then is convinced that he has lapsed into a deep sleep. He is not taking a nap; he is hiding in order not to be drawn down one of those roads that lead nowhere. It is the sleep of fear. The heart is still beating strongly enough to prevent one from slipping into unconsciousness. It's unpleasant sleep, disturbed and redoubtable. The anguish derives from the fact that one can still hear all the things going on in one's body: breathing, heartbeat, pulse. The body is an old machine susceptible at any moment of breaking down.

Someone is knocking at the door. He raises his

head and squints. The cleaning woman goes to answer. It's Krimo, a taxi driver who stops by from time to time to offer his services. A native of the Rif, a rather nervous man, he enters the room, dripping from the rain. He removes his shoes and bows, offering his greetings:

"I thought you might need a ride—in view of the weather."

"What's the weather got to do with it? I told you not to come back. I can still get around on foot. I go to my shop twice a day. Unless you've come to talk to me a little in Riffian . . . I learned that language at the same time as Spanish. A beautiful language. A little rough, maybe, like the country, but direct, almost brutally direct."

"It's your son who pays me for this; you know that, sir. I'll continue to stop by now and then, and you can do as you please. As for the Rif, I haven't set foot in those parts for twenty years."

"Like you, my son thinks I've reached the age when I have to be transported in a little car."

"What I'm proposing is not a little car, sir, but a diesel-powered Mercedes 200, specially imported from Germany for your personal service."

"Ah, that's another matter! Have a seat, my friend; have a cup of coffee. The coffee is imported from Brazil and is roasted in Spain. It will perk you up."

"No, thank you. I don't drink coffee. And besides, I don't have much time. In weather like this, they don't give us a moment's rest."

"So let's say you're working, you're driving me to the shop. That's enough time for a cup of coffee and a cigarette. We've just left. Lean back and relax, my friend; tell me a funny story. Because with a face like yours, if you can't make your customers laugh, you're finished. Either the taxi will stall in the middle of the street or bad luck will overtake your customers!"

The man laughs, takes a seat, and pours himself a cup of coffee.

"So here we are, on rue de Mexique, waiting for the light to change. In ten minutes, I must be in calle Tétouan. Here's a story about a miser . . ."

"Ah, misers! The offspring of the Devil! I know them well; they're my mortal enemies. Between them and me there's been more than one serious fight. We can't stand the sight of each other. I always recognize them. When a miser offers you his hand, he's apt to snatch it back, afraid of losing something."

"A story about a miser who's just lost his mother, who is telling his friends about it. 'Poor me! She died and left me!' 'What did she have?' asks one of his friends. 'Oh, nothing much: a necklace and a gold bracelet . . .' "

"A terrible joke! I don't find it the least bit funny. That man had no idea of the respect due a parent. Without our parents' blessings, we would suffer bad fortune in this life, and we would run the risk of God's punishment in the next. I always had my parents' blessing. And I never hesitated to bestow my

93

blessing on my children, even when they fell short of their duty to me. That's how I am. Because when I was young, I saw how my mother suffered when my older brother left Fez the day after his marriage, taking himself off to Melilla to seek his fortune. For eleven years, we had no news from him. Eleven years of absence and anguish! We didn't even have his address. We didn't know if he was in Nador or Melilla. In those days, you remember, communication between French-occupied Morocco and Spanish-occupied Morocco was not very good. My mother lost her youth during that long wait. It wasn't the waiting that aged her; it was the sickness that came from it. One day, she sent my other brother and me to the edge of the city, to a sort of wild garden, an abandoned place where the natives of Fez hardly ever went. It was called the Witches' Garden. It had a spring—really a well, not very deep. If I remember right, it went by the name Aïn Ben Diab. Legend said it was the well of the lost ones. All you had to do was go there at dusk, the hour when the light is uncertain, and shout the name of the one you're waiting for. You called the name in a loud, clear voice, then you listened. If there was no echo, it was because the person had heard you. That's how it worked. I didn't have much faith in it myself, but because our mother had begun to see her son everywhere, and seemed on the verge of going crazy, we did what she told us to. I don't know if our calls were heard, but one morning a few months later, just at dawn, the absent one returned. When my mother saw him, she thought she was dreaming. She smiled and fainted, not having said a word to him. She died soon afterward, from sadness."

"Well, Krimo, you can go now. We've reached our destination. As you can see, we've just passed calle Tétouan. You can drop me here on the corner. Go, with my blessing!"

Heavy silence hangs over the house. He takes out his wallet and counts the money in it: 152 dirhams. He re-counts it, suspecting that he has been robbed. He is certain there were five 100-dirham notes in there. He paid the telephone bill: 308 dirhams. So what happened to the other 40 dirhams? Oh, it's the price of a box of suppositories. That's it; he forgot that he'd thrown them away. Cursing medicine and his illness, he slips the wallet beneath his pillow and tries to sleep. But he isn't the least bit sleepy. He gets up and goes to the kitchen to put the kettle on. He will make the tea himself. In his impatience, he gets the proportions wrong and very nearly scalds himself with the boiling water. But the tea comforts him, allowing him to feel a little less lonely.

How can a man change the passage of time? How can he emerge unscathed from such an interminable day? He looks around. Nothing has moved. Yet in his head there is such a bustle, such incessant coming and going, such commotion, that he knows it won't be long before he has another headache. He is subject to migraines. He can't remember when the first one struck him. He says, with resignation, that he must have been born with a headache, just as others are born with a sixth finger. He has tried all the known remedies: aspirin and the other painkillers, as well as traditional panaceas like applying a slice of potato to the brow and holding it there with a handkerchief.

With age, the headaches have become less insistent, less intense. Today, it is the memory of earlier headaches that causes him pain; the mere thought of them makes him tremble. He is astonished to discover that the memory of a pain can also be painful. He tries not to think of the commotion in his head; he tries to banish all unpleasant memories. "It is a question of heredity," he tells himself. His migraines, like his powers of observation and his obsession with finding fault, were faithfully passed on from father to son. He remembers how his father used to sit with his head in his hands, and his sons often complained of that pain. They have all spent their lives doing battle with an army of sharp little needles that attack the nerve ends beneath the skull with punctual regularity.

The address book is open. He flips through it, absentmindedly. His finger comes to rest on the name Zrirek. He smiles. At last, a ray of hope. Zrirek is his barber. His nickname comes from his blue eyes. He is a small man, as sly as a fox, a man who knows everything about everybody, who can recount the life story of every man and woman in the quarter. He claims to have a list of all the children born of adulterous relationships. When he was younger, he performed circumcisions; he kept the thumbnail on his right hand long and sharp, so he could make a mark on the foreskin before cutting it with a pair of scissors. Zrirek is an amusing man, but he has a wicked tongue and is not to be trusted. He speaks ill of everyone, but he does it in such a lighthearted tone that no one takes offense. He is a master of ironic understatement. He says that all he is doing is dressing up the truth, clothing it in a gold-embroidered caftan.

"Could you stop by a little later to give me a trim?"

"Are you sure you have any hair left?"

He passes a hand over his skull. A few rebellious hairs still cling there. He counts them. Nineteen.

He waits patiently for Zrirek, but under no delusion.

"No more hair! What a desert! But isn't that the sign of a thinking man, a mind that never stops working? I didn't lose my hair overnight. It's because of all the ideas that are forever jostling one another in my head, trying to clear a path into the open. With each storm, a few more hairs have fallen."

It isn't the barber who comes, but Bouida the iron-monger. They call him Bouida because of his egg-shaped face. He's inclined to fidget; he can't sit still.

He's a distant cousin, a man with several wives and a number of children. He has trouble feeding them all, but he never complains. When he learned one day that one of his daughters had turned to prostitution, he suffered a stroke. Now, he has difficulty shaping his words; he has to communicate with his eyes, which are full of pain and compassion. Even when he smiles, there is a quality of sadness in his look. He tries to sit still in his chair, because he knows that it irritates people to see him fidget. He removes two apples from his bag.

"You know I can't eat apples! You know I have no teeth! Never mind; thanks, I'll give them to my wife."

Their conversation resembles that of two deaf-mutes. This amuses them. They sip their tea. Bouida fills his pipe with kef and lights it, but when he sees that the smoke bothers his sick friend, he puts out the pipe, kisses him on the brow, and leaves, trying hard not to fidget.

What he would like is to have a good wash, just as in the old days: to spend an entire morning in the hammam, to scrub himself from head to toe, to stretch out and relax, to take his time over his ablutions, to nap in the lounge. He allows himself to dream of these things, knowing that he wouldn't be able to tolerate the heat and the steam. Since his first asthma attack, the hammam has been forbidden to him. At first, he tried to create a similar atmosphere at home, but without success; he was not able to wash himself properly, and he couldn't get used to the shower. These days, he has to fill the bath with hot water and stretch out in it. His wife has to help him. But instead of responding kindly to her services, he abuses her. He doesn't like to be dependent on others.

His wife is a *sherifa*, a direct descendant of the Prophet Muhammad. If she wanted to, she could become a saint. She is known for her healing powers, her ability to ward off the evil eye and to exorcise its spell once it has been cast. How often has he depended on her urgent intervention when he felt himself becoming feverish and weary—two sure signs of the evil eye. Armed with a bay twig whose leaves have been singed in the fire, she chants prayers until she feels the evil emerging from the exhausted body and entering her own, disappearing finally in an effusion of yawns and tears. To rid oneself of the evil eye once and for all, it is necessary to remunerate the *sherifa*, with either a small coin or a pinch of salt. He always "pays" her with salt, though he knows she would prefer a more generous offering.

Despite his innate skepticism and his passion for science, he has always preferred to be treated with these old wives' remedies—though, in his opinion, their effect lies entirely in the mind of the patient, who only imagines himself to be sick.

He reopens the address book. His eye falls upon

the name Hassan (314 21 and 364 50), followed by the name Hussein. They are twins, childhood friends whom he hasn't seen in years. Then, just as he's dialing the number, he remembers that one of them died in a car accident. He no longer knows which one.

"Well, there's nothing unusual about that; they always looked so much alike. We went to Koran classes together. Everyone had difficulty telling them apart. They used to drive the schoolmaster crazy. Needless to say, they took advantage of this. I liked them both, but we lost sight of each other. They, too, ran aground in this damp, windy city. They made a fortune in the fifties on American army surplus goods. But how can I find out which one is still alive? I can't very well call and ask if it was Hussein or Hassan who was struck by a truck on the road to Casablanca. Perhaps I could make a joke of my error? But I don't have the heart to do that. So here I am, deprived not just of one friend, but of two. What a loss! It seems like a conspiracy.

"What if I were to call Moshé, my former neighbor? He's no longer in the fabric business; he switched to something else—real estate, I think. But it's been such a long time since I last saw him. I suppose I could always call his office. Perhaps I would discover that he has gone to Canada or France. I'm sure he didn't emigrate to Israel. He was about to leave in June of 1967, but he changed his mind. He spent the entire month of June in Gibraltar, waiting for the war between the Jews and the Arabs to end. But he said he would never be able to leave his country, particularly after hearing of the misfortunes of his cousins and friends who had abandoned everything to go and live in Israel and who were disappointed with the paradise that had been promised them there. Moshé is a good man; I'm sorry I didn't keep in touch with him. I wonder what has become of him. He's probably a happy grandfather, shut up in his house, confined to his bed, but surrounded by his children and his grandchildren. Has he lost all his friends, too? Is he the last of his group? Did he watch them all die, one after the other? I can see him crossing their names out in his address book, gradually, reluctant to find himself alone without warning.

"To think that I always looked upon myself as an organized man! Well, so I am. But my list of names has always been centered on my family, not my friends. As a result of having devoted my attention to the family tree, I have neglected that of friendship. And yet I always felt more sympathy for my friends than for my relatives. Rarely have I looked upon a cousin as a friend. That said, I always insisted that the family's bonds remain strong, though more out of duty than love. Before dying, our father made us promise not to lose touch with one another. I followed his instruction faithfully, but I believe I was the only one to do so. I often have the impression that I've spent my life assembling the pieces of an impossible puzzle, that someday I may even discover that I've been working with the wrong pieces and on the wrong puzzle. He might have spared us such a futile task; he might have insisted that we spend our lives traveling to faraway places or engaging in some difficult study. But no, he preferred to leave us in the mediocrity of our businesses, to deprive us of ambition, to burden us with the duty to remain united. Now, more than half a century later, we are still not united and not one of us has made a fortune. We never left Morocco. If it weren't for our children, upon whom we have depended to save our name, we would be doomed to extinction. I'm proud of my sons. But are they proud of me? There are days when I doubt it. They take the side of their mother, rushing to her defense before she is attacked. I have learned to live with this favoritism, but it pains me nonetheless; sometimes it even brings tears to my eyes. Do they realize how unjust and partial they are? The engineer, for example, worries more about his children's health than about his father's. That's normal. But the other one is completely under his mother's thumb. He treats me very unfairly. I would like to be closer to him, to be able to discuss things with him. I would like him to tell me about his trips, his successes; but I am reduced to learning most of what I know about him from the newspapers and the neighbors. I would like to be his friend, his confidant, his counselor, but he never comes to me for advice, he never consults me on anything. We have never had a serious discussion. If I ask him questions, he is content to reply yes or no. He is resentful of me, I know. Still, I'm proud of my two children. Both of them, the engineer and the artist, are loved and respected. I've tried to make them understand the importance of maintaining close family ties, but they are reluctant to follow me in this matter. Who knows? Perhaps they're right.

"In some places, old people are housed in a separate building, a nice building with neat little garden and clean nurses to look after them. Not like here, where the nurse chews gum and stinks of sweat. When she leans over me to give me a shot, I have to hold my nose. If they had something like that here, it would not be a rest home, but a chicken coop for senile old men who still entertain illusions about the human condition. Fortunately, the people who run our country haven't caught on to the idea of putting their elders away. Perhaps that's why our cemeteries are more attractive than those in Europe; they're open, unconfined, surrounded by fields of wild grasses. As a rule, the dead are buried on a hill overlooking the city. There are some who even say that the dead are watching over us. But whether on a sunny hillside covered with olive trees or in a fenced plot paved with marble, the earth is the earth. It has the same taste, it is saturated with the same moisture, it harbors the same insects, the same worms, the same roots. The location makes no difference. Sunlight makes no difference. Go and ask the stones which they prefer, to be hammered by the rain or scorched by the blinding sun.

"A dream—I had a troubling dream. It came a while ago, when I was halfway between sleep and waking. I must talk about it, if I want to forget it. It was one of those insistent dreams that confuses itself with reality. I dreamed that I was dead. Suddenly, the family came running. The relatives from Fez arrived before those from Casablanca. Afternoon prayers were over, but still I wasn't buried. They were awaiting the arrival of the latecomers. At this point, I revived. No one was surprised. I participated in the discussion concerning arrangements for my funeral. I expressed a desire to be buried in Fez. This posed certain problems for my children, who have never liked that city. I insisted, as is my habit. There was very little sorrow in the air. They found it quite normal that I should have a say in the matter; no one took issue with me. But perhaps they couldn't see me or hear me at all. I moved from one to the other. No one showed the least astonishment or fear. Even dead, I believe I'll continue to express my opinion and to resist any attempt on the part of others to ignore it. That is the distinct impression I have left from this dream.

"As I was unraveling this dream, my wife entered

the room, nervous and agitated. She announced that her younger brother, the one she always loved so dearly and who died five years ago, had come looking for her. Everything in her dream was white, she said. He approached and stretched out a hand in her direction, an infallible sign that she must put her affairs in order. When she proceeded to get out a clean white sheet embroidered with white flowers, I became frightened. She spread it out in the room, to air it, she said, to remove the musty odor. It lay between us like a shroud. I have made no such preparations myself. Indeed, I am inclined to scoff at religious women who go so far as to send their shroud to spend the night in Mecca or to lie on the tomb of Muhammad in Medina. Women, especially as they grow older, feel drawn to make arrangements with the beyond. Sometimes, at the end of her prayers, I hear my wife speaking directly to God. It's so naive—like the petty calculations of a grocer who has nothing to sell. These things make me laugh, I must confess. And the more I laugh, the more irritated she becomes. I like to annoy her, because she has no sense of humor.

"But it seems to me she is less apprehensive of death than I am. I often hear her speaking of it, calmly and with resignation. She expects to be reunited with her mother and her brothers on the far side. As for me, I don't intend to be reunited with anyone, not my friends, not my parents. Consequently, my solitude weighs even more heavily on me. It is intensified by the thought that it will be eternal. All the same, I prefer to face facts. I'm not going to follow the example of the Japanese, and have myself deposited on a mat at the top of Toubkal, there to await death by hunger and exposure, if I should be fortunate enough to escape the claws of rapacious birds. That the ants may devour my flesh once I am beneath the earth does not trouble me in the least, but that birds of prey should pluck out my eyes while I'm still alive—that, I find intolerable! At the same time, I find the idea rather amusing. People would say, 'Oh, he's not dead; he's just gone to the mountain!' They would count the days, they would check the weather forecasts, they would conclude that a man might hold out for at least twenty days and nights under the circumstances. But I don't suppose this way of death is practiced any longer in Japan; the Japanese are more inclined to commit suicide. Such a thing is forbidden in our country. Both life and death belong to God. He takes back what He gave when it suits Him to do so. I prefer this version. Real or imaginary, the notion has something logical about it. As for heaven and hell, everyone has his own idea about them. If hell exists, I know some people I wouldn't hesitate to consign to it. Like that gang of bullies who used to torment me because I had trouble walking. I'll never forget how that fifteen-year-old, blind in one eye, yanked the hood of my djellaba one day and made me fall; and the laughter of his friends lurking nearby. I did my best to defend myself with my cane. I was humiliated. But I refused to register a complaint with the police, because I was afraid they would redouble their assaults and do me some permanent damage. I never told my sons about that episode. What a disgrace, to see your father groveling helplessly, surrounded by terrorists! Oh, I have no trouble imagining that riffraff in hell. I prefer for myself the hell of life. Still, I hope to see them condemned to perdition someday.

"As for heaven, I was convinced that I had a glimpse of it one day when I was twenty. I was standing in the middle of a green, red, and yellow field, facing an immense door, which was slightly ajar. On the other side of the door was an open space, in which a number of girls in thin dresses were riding bicycles. On that day, a single tear, one only, fell on my cheek. I had experienced a moment of bliss."

The rain has stopped. The wind has died down. The cafés of the quarter are filled; their windows are steamed over. It is difficult to make out the figures inside, but it is possible to hear the clamor of voices. A soccer match must be in progress. In Tangier, many homes can receive both Spanish and English television channels. Those who can't afford the necessary antenna gather in a café, not to talk, but to follow the matches. They respond to each play with the same enthusiasm or the same anger they would show if they were seated in the stadium.

Listening intently, he hears a loud cry of joy: Hurray!

He would like to be a part of that crowd of people who lose their heads over a mere ball. He doesn't understand their passion, but just once he would like to be a part of it. It is something he has never experienced. And he doesn't like to find himself in situations in which he cannot comprehend what is going on. For the moment, he must make do with the faint cry that reaches him here in his room. He puts his head in his hands and covers his ears. He doesn't like games; they're too risky, too dangerous. That's why he settled in Tangier, a quiet city in a state of decline, rather than Casablanca, a bustling, up-and-coming place.

"I must stop thinking. That's it: I'm not going to think anymore. I'm going to create space around me. I'm going to empty my mind of everything, shut out the little demons that threaten my tranquillity, banish my obsessions. The wind seems less violent now though it's still strong enough to open the window and the door. I get out of bed. The air feels less humid, almost pleasant. There's a warm wind coming out of the north. The sky is clear. It has changed color since I last looked at it. Where did all the clouds go? The sky is blue. It's a lovely day. Summer has arrived. It must be siesta time, because there are few people in the streets. I go down rue Quévedo. The light is so strong I have to squint. A girl passes me on a bicycle. The wind lifts her skirt and plays in her hair. I can see her legs. They're superb. She smiles at me. I stop and wait. She turns, gets off her bicycle, and moves toward me. I don't say a word. I am intrigued by her smile. Her face is not unfamiliar. Where have I seen it before? Perhaps she is only a mirage, a vision of grace and light. Perhaps she is only a dazzling, delightful apparition. But I am not dreaming. I feel the gentle touch of the wind on my face. I hear distant singing. Is this what it's like to stop thinking? I don't say a word. She offers me the bicycle. It's brand-new. I climb on it, hoping not to lose my balance. But I have no difficulty keeping upright. With agility, the girl seats herself on the bar between the saddle and the handlebars. I lower my head to her left shoulder. Her hair blows gently in my face as we roll through a field flooded with light and mirrors."